To my
and loving friend, Amy ...

♡ Molly
McLain

SECRET

MASON CREEK

USA TODAY BESTSELLING AUTHOR
# MOLLY McLAIN

Cover Designer: Opium House Cover Designs

Cover Photo License: Depositphotos

Editing & Proofreading: My Brother's Editor

❀ Created with Vellum

*To my husband.*
*Until we can visit Montana for real...*

# PROLOGUE

*FOUR YEARS EARLIER...*

"$\mathcal{I}$'m done with men. In fact, from now on, I'm a lesbian."

From the stool beside me at Pony Up's glossy mahogany bar, Laken laughs. "Oh, sweetie, you don't want to do that. Toys are nice, but nothing compares to a real life dick."

"Ugh. Dicks are nothing but trouble. T-r-o-u-b-l-e. Especially the ones attached to cheating, no good bull riders." I reach for my drink, but it's empty. Dammit, who drank it when I wasn't looking?

"The one attached to Cory Mitchell is the absolute worst, but I wouldn't write off all men, Al. Most are pretty decent. Take Aiden, for example." Emma bats her eyelashes and purses her lips, and I almost throw up. I've been away from Mason Creek for almost three years, but she's still just as gaga over my brother as she's always been.

"Eww. Do not bring Aiden into this." I lift my empty glass in the air to catch the attention of the bartender. Maybe if I have just one more drink, I'll forget she said that. Maybe I'll forget about Cory, too.

"Already?" Jack strolls over with a smirk to go along with his cowboy swagger.

"Yep. Fill me up, handsome!"

"Won't be able to say that again if you become a lesbian now, will you?" Jessie snarks and Jack's brows dart up.

"Who's a lesbian? Alana?"

"Yep. Mason Creek's golden boy turned me into one. I never want to see another dick in my life."

He chuckles and takes my glass, adding a scoop of ice before the Malibu. "Not sure 'golden boy' is the correct term. Douche canoe, maybe. Sack of dog shit, for sure."

"How is it that everyone knew he was bad news but me?" Maybe I should have come home from college more often. Maybe they would have clued me in, not that I would have listened.

"Love makes us blind." Laken sighs and Emma nods along.

"She's right," Jack says, topping off my drink with pineapple juice. "Don't let an asshole like that make you shut up shop and miss out on all the fun. You're young yet. Hell, you're just starting out."

Starting out? Nah, I've taken a few too many steps backward for that. At twenty-one, I should be spending the summer interning and planning my future, not back home nursing a broken heart and suddenly questioning everything.

For four years, I built my life around Cory. My high school sweetheart and the man who'd promised we'd grow old together on a ranch right here in Mason Creek once he retired from bull riding.

But instead, he broke every promise he'd ever made to me in a single weekend. With not just one girl... not even two... but three. Three buckle bunnies in as many days.

And just like that, everything I thought to be true about my life came crashing down around me.

And he didn't just tell me about it—he bragged. Like I was supposed to be as proud of him for breaking my heart as I was him adding another buckle to his collection.

Maybe all men aren't lying, cheating scumbags, and maybe I'm not really going to become a lesbian, but I will never—and I mean never—so much as look at a man in cowboy boots and chaps again.

And I will absolutely never—tie me to a stake and set me on fire never—fall for another bull rider.

# CHAPTER 1

ALANA

"*P*lease tell me you're joking."

Old Man Morton shakes his head of thick white hair. "Sorry, Al. Wilder is having his cabins at the ranch renovated before the rodeo comes to town next month, and the kid needs a place to stay."

"But there's no bathroom." And frankly the tiny room across from my apartment above the Mason Creek Market is hardly fit for a closet, let alone a place to live. It's barely the size of a dorm room, for Pete's sake.

"He's not picky. Besides, he'll be using your bathroom."

I nearly drop the cash register drawer I just spent twenty minutes reconciling to the grocery store's black and white tiled floor.

"You can't be serious." Share my bathroom with a complete stranger? A guy, no less. Who, from the sounds of it, is some random fly-by-night Wilder took pity upon.

"No offense, kiddo, but you live here almost rent-free. Have for more than four years now. Sharing your bathroom

4

with the young man for a short while isn't going to kill you."

Maybe not, but this *young man*, whoever he is, might just kill *me*.

"Do you know anything about this person, Marty? Anything at all?" I lower my voice as Susie, the service desk clerk for the afternoon, returns from her break and comes around the counter. She's as nosy as they come, and I'd kind of like to wrap my head around the bomb Marty just dropped on me before the whole town hears.

Marty lifts a shoulder covered in red and black flannel, despite it being one of the hottest days in August. "No, but if he's a friend of Aiden and Wilder, he's probably a decent guy."

*Probably*. No doubt Jeffrey Dahmer's neighbors thought he was a *probably* nice guy at one point, too.

Setting the drawer on the counter, I curl an arm around my waist as my stomach begins to twist and turn. "I wish you would have talked to me about this before you told Wilder it was okay."

"Actually, I told Aiden it was okay. He asked for Wilder since he was too busy at the ranch to come into town himself."

"Wait—my brother was in on this?" I think I'm going to be sick.

Marty lifts a hand. "Again, I'm real sorry for the inconvenience, but I couldn't very well say no when Aiden asked. The kid is due to arrive in town any minute and Wilder was in a bind."

So, putting me in a bind to make Wilder's life easier seemed like the right decision? Wow. Clearly, my brother didn't mention this to Emma, his lady love and one of my best friends, or she would have set him straight ASAP.

"Can you put the drawer away for me?" I ask Susie, who's

openly eavesdropping, her eyes volleying back and forth between me and Marty like a ball. I wouldn't be surprised if she calls Hattie and Hazel Jackson to report the new development as soon as I leave. "I suddenly don't feel so well. I think I need to lie down."

"Sure thing, Alana. You want me to lock up tonight's drawers too so you don't have to come down?"

"Yes, please. Just in case."

"It's only for a few weeks," Marty adds as I grab my backpack, make sure my cell phone is tucked inside, and sling it over my shoulder with a heavy sigh.

"Mmm hmm." A few weeks too many. "What time is this *kid* supposed to be here exactly?"

"Not sure. I have some errands to run real quick, and then I'll be back to move some things around in his apartment. You might want to make some space for our guest in that bathroom. Put some of your girly stuff away and whatnot."

Yeah, I don't think so. If I'm going to be forced to share my private space with some wandering ranch hand, he can deal with my stuff just like it is.

"See you tomorrow, Susie," I mutter and then make a quick trek to the back of the Mason Creek Market, past the frozen foods section and into the storage area with shelves full of extra dry and canned goods, and to the staircase that leads to my apartment upstairs.

Marty's right—I have lived here for four years and I haven't paid actual rent or even had to contribute to the utilities, for that matter. But that's only because it was part of the deal we struck when I took the job managing the store. I get paid for forty hours, but I put in no less than sixty on any given week. I never take days off and, besides my online college classes, I live and breathe the Mason Creek Market.

I may not financially contribute to the store, but I keep it running and have since I came back to Mason Creek. In fact,

I make most of the decisions around here, so the fact that Marty didn't think to include me on this one? It's frustrating. And also a humbling reminder that as much work as I put in here, the market isn't mine. And, if my savings account is any indication, it won't ever be.

Dropping my backpack into a side chair in the living room, I stalk straight to my bedroom and face-plant on the mattress.

I need to come up with another plan to get the money to buy the store, because that 'for sale' sign is going to go up in the front window any day now. Marty's been talking about it forever and, at seventy-six, he's not messing around.

HOLDEN

"You beat me here!" Aiden Faulkner laughs from the open window in his police cruiser as he pulls into the back lot of the Mason Creek Market a couple of minutes after me.

"And to think I drove around town a couple of times, too." Tucking my hands into my jeans, I grin. "You get tied up with your girl, or what?"

He chuckles as he hops out. "Nah, just had to stop for gas."

"Uh huh." Pretty sure that lipstick on his cheek wasn't there a few minutes earlier when I'd met him at Pony Up to discuss my living accommodations, but since we don't know each other well, I'll pretend I don't see it. "Nice little town you've got here."

"She's pretty sweet, isn't she? Just wait until the leaves start changing in a few weeks."

"Yeah, I should still be around then." Unless something

7

drastic changes and CJ says I can come back to the rodeo circuit sooner, but I'm not holding my breath.

"Old Man Morton said he'd be upstairs moving some stuff around, so let's head on in and see what's what." Aiden tips his head toward the steel door marked 'for business only' beside a larger delivery door at the back of the old brick building.

"Thanks again for hooking me up with this. Wilder forgot about his cabins being renovated when he invited me up."

"No problem at all. In fact, most people don't know this room even exists. I only do because my sister lives in the apartment across the hall." He presses a code into the security panel and the door clicks open. "5-7-7-2, by the way. For future reference."

"Got it." I smirk and follow him inside, where it takes my eyes a second to adjust to the dark space. It's only lit by a couple emergency lights and it's obviously a storage space, given the shelving and the relic of a forklift parked just inside the delivery door.

"There are other lights, but Marty—aka Old Man Morton — likes to keep 'em off to save electricity. The switch is right here if you need it." Aiden thumbs to a panel by the door and then nods to the staircase. "Your room is up this way."

"So, you said your sister lives here, too?" I ask, following after him.

"Yep. Her name is Alana. She also manages the grocery store, so it's convenient. And you shouldn't have any problems with her. She's either working or doing homework."

"Ah, she's in college?" Probably young. Hopefully not annoying.

"Uh huh. Almost done, too. Took her a little longer than normal because of some life shit, but she's a good egg. Now, anyway."

"Now?"

"Yeah, she left Mason Creek for college but ended up coming back when she got her heart broken. You might know a little something about that." He glances over his shoulder when we hit the top of the steps and, yeah, I know all about shitty relationships. "Anyway, she went a little wild for a few months and then she did a one-eighty overnight. Now, we can't get her to loosen up for anything."

"Huh." Sounds like she'll be quiet, at least. Not that I plan to be around a lot. I hope like hell Wilder keeps me busy enough at the ranch so these few weeks of not-so-voluntary sequestration go by quickly.

"Aiden, is that you?" a raspy, somewhat breathless voice calls from down a short hall, covered in old school, faux wood paneling. "Come on back."

"That'd be the old man," Aiden murmurs as we head down the hall that has a total of three doors. The first one on the left ahead is open, but the two on the right are closed. One of them has a floral wreath hanging on it.

"Your sister's place?" I jut my chin toward the flowers and tuck my hands into my pockets.

"Yeah. I'll introduce you to her before I head out. In case you need anything."

"Sounds good." Again, I don't plan on needing much, but I should probably make nice with the neighbor just in case.

"There you are." An old man with thick white hair, a burly middle covered flannel, and sweat across his forehead glances up when Aiden and I enter the room. Aiden had warned me it was small, so I'm not surprised that it looks like a prison cell minus the toilet in the corner.

"Hey, Marty. Looks like you've been busy," Aiden says, hurrying ahead to help adjust a tall dresser back against the wall.

"Oh, just rearranging some things to make it more welcoming. Haven't had anyone stay here before, but it turns out I had almost an entire bedroom set from home up here in storage."

The twin bed is older, for sure, but it's well-kept and there's a stack of clean bedding on a small table in the corner with a single chair. There's also the dresser, a side table, and a mini-fridge with a small TV sitting on top.

"Marty, this is Holden. Holden, Marty." Aiden waves a hand between us, and I step forward to shake the man's hand.

"I appreciate you letting me bunk here a few weeks." I'd much rather be at home in Colorado in my own bed, but since the media figured out where I lived, sticking around wasn't really an option.

"No problem at all." The old man props his hands on his hips and takes a moment to catch his breath. "Well, there might be one small problem."

"What's that?" I ask. I can see I'm going to need a coffee pot and more pillows, but I'd already expected I'd have to pick up a few things.

"I'm afraid there's only one bathroom up here."

Aiden grimaces. "Shit, I forgot about that."

"Alana said she'd clean up her stuff, so it shouldn't be a problem," the old man adds.

Hold up. "I'll be sharing a bathroom with your sister?" I glance to Aiden, mostly in surprise, but partly to make sure he's okay with it. He's a friend of a friend and we've met a few times over the years, but we're not close. For all he knows, I'm some creepy closet asshole.

"Yeah." His face twists almost guiltily, obviously more concerned about my comfort than his sister's. "Sorry about that. It completely slipped my mind."

"No worries, man." I mean, I don't know the girl, but I grew up sharing a bathroom with my younger brother and sister. Can't be worse than that, right? "As long as she's okay with it, that's all that matters."

Marty nods adamantly. "She will be."

Will be? Does she not know yet? "Maybe I should meet her."

The old man pulls in a breath and lets it out with a resigned huff. "I suppose we should do that. Let's head over."

Aiden waves a hand toward the hall and I lead the way to the door with the floral wreath. Marty steps in front of me, rapping his knuckles against the wood for a solid two minutes before an annoyed feminine voice calls from the other side.

"For the love of God, Marty, I'm coming!"

Yeah, this isn't going to go well.

I brace myself for the wrath of this mystery woman as the door jerks open and the sexiest pair of hazel eyes I've ever seen land on mine.

She scowls—no, correct that… she physically grimaces—and promptly shifts her gaze from me to Marty. "I told you earlier that I didn't feel well," she says calmly, but there's no denying the edge to her tone. "I was sleeping."

"Sorry, kiddo, but I wanted to introduce you to your new neighbor."

She rolls her eyes, tucks a lock of silky auburn hair behind her ear, and crosses her arms over her chest… But not before I catch a glimpse of her nipples tightening beneath her T-shirt.

Sexy eyes, a mouth full of sass, and no bra. Good Lord. I should feel bad that she already hates me, but I'm more intrigued than anything.

"I'm Holden." I lean around Marty and offer my hand. Those coppery eyes flick down to the gesture while she sucks in her cheeks and resists.

"What the hell is your problem, Al?" Aiden snaps behind me.

Her gaze swings to him and her nostrils flare. "Would have been nice if you'd have given me a heads-up about this."

He scoffs. "Wasn't like I had much notice."

"It takes two seconds to send a text."

"You're right. And maybe I would have if I wasn't working. You know, keeping this town safe for pleasant citizens such as yourself."

Those gorgeous eyes narrow before she lifts her chin and finally looks at me. She doesn't take my hand, though, so I let it drop and offer a smile instead.

"I promise not to be a pain in your ass. In fact, I'll probably spend most of my time out at Wilder's. You won't even know I'm here."

"Too late for that." She searches my face for a long moment before lifting her chin a little higher. "There are two doors to the bathroom. One inside my apartment and the one in the hall. I'll lock the hall door from the inside when I'm using it. If it's unlocked, it's free. And don't even think about touching the inside door. Ever."

Wow. Am I giving off asshole vibes or is she really this uptight?

"Fair enough." I dip my chin and leave it at that. For now. I'm typically not the kind of guy who's bothered by other people's opinion of me, but something about her thinking I'm a dick rubs me the wrong way. Maybe it's the fact that the entire reason I'm even here in Mason Creek is because I've been accused of doing something I didn't and her judgment is like salt in a wound.

Or maybe it's because she's really friggin' pretty and something about that amber gaze of hers tells me there's more to this girl than meets the eye.

# CHAPTER 2

ALANA

*I* have a bad feeling about this.

It's been two hours since Marty and Aiden ambushed me at the door with the new guy, but I still can't shake the feeling that there's more to this than anyone is telling me.

So I call Emma for the scoop.

"Hey, girl!" she answers on the third ring and the line is immediately filled with loud country music and laughter. "I'm at the bar right now. Can't talk unless you want to come down and have a drink with me."

"Ugh, that would require getting dressed." My stomach has settled from earlier, and while a drink doesn't really appeal, a greasy bar cheeseburger does. "I am hungry though."

"Well, get your butt down here and I'll feed you. Extra fries and all."

My belly growls and I smile. "Girl, you know the way to my heart. I'll see you in a half hour."

"I'll save you a barstool!" she sings and hangs up.

I spend the next few minutes making myself presentable in the bathroom, all the while eyeing the door that I'm begrudgingly going to have to unlock when I'm done.

Who the heck is this guy, anyway? And why is he really here? It matters little that Aiden and Marty are willing to back his credibility, because I've known them both long enough to know their judgment isn't always as up to par as they'd like to think.

The only solace I have at the moment is that this guy—Holden, I think he said his name was—didn't look like the punk kid I was expecting. And he didn't look like a strung out wanderer, either.

But just because he looks like the kind of small-town guy I see in the store and around town on a regular basis doesn't mean that's what he is. I've been fooled by wolves in sheep's clothing before.

Yet, I don't really have a choice but to give him a chance. With my bathroom, that is. I definitely don't plan to get to know him. In fact, I plan to do everything I can to avoid him and hope these next few weeks go by quickly.

Sighing, I flip the lock on the door between the bathroom and the hall and head downtown to Pony Up.

"Alana Banana!" Emma calls from behind the bar when she spots me. A few locals turn my way as well, raising their mugs in greeting. By the time I claim the seat Emma has saved for me at the far end of the bar, she's already setting a can of Diet Dr. Pepper and a glass of ice in front of me. "From Jessie and Doc."

"Aww." I scan the bar and find them sitting at a booth with their son Parker. Jessie is a couple years older than me and, while we used to be close, our friendship isn't what it used to be. If I'm honest, I've always been a little jealous of her. She's independent as heck and she worked her butt off earning a business degree and putting it to good use when she opened Java Jitters, the best darn coffee shop this town has ever seen.

I'll be done with school next April, but I'm down to my final three classes—two this upcoming fall semester and one during the spring term. I'm proud of how far I've come on my degree after taking time off when things went to crap with Cory. But it's the business owner part that worries me. I want what Jessie has—a place to call my own—but I have no idea how the heck I'm going to afford it.

"So, Aiden said he was by your place earlier," Emma says while grabbing a bottle of beer for a guy who sauntered over from the pool table.

"Ugh. He sure was." I pour my soda into the glass and sigh. "Did he happen to tell you why?"

"Something about a guy staying across the hall from you. A ranch hand of Wilder and Levi's, right?" She hands over the beer and collects the guy's money before turning back to me.

"Apparently. I know Wilder's having his cabins renovated, so I get that he doesn't have the room to put this guy up, but why the store? Why my little piece of privacy, you know?"

She tosses her long blonde hair over her shoulder and presses her lips together into an appeasing smile. "I get it. Especially with the whole bathroom thing. I mean, I'd be just as annoyed."

"Thank you for that. Old Man Morton and Aiden looked at me like I was crazy and for a few minutes I started to wonder if I was."

"Nah, girl, you have every right to be skeptical. I mean, I'd be nervous enough having a new neighbor let alone one like him." She props her elbows on the bar and leans in, waggling her eyebrows. "I heard he's hot," she whispers. "But don't tell your brother I said that."

I snort and roll my eyes. "Who told you that?"

"Laken who heard it from Sadie who saw Hallie at Jessie's coffee shop earlier today."

So, the town is already talking. I'm not surprised, it's just… "He's not that hot."

Emma's eyes narrow and she searches my face for a long beat before smirking. "You are such a horrible liar, Alana Faulkner."

"I'm not lying. He's just a guy." A broad-shouldered, built-like-a-cowboy guy with unruly dark blond hair and smoldering brown eyes. Under normal circumstances, I might have taken an extra moment to appreciate his God-given assets—after all, I'm single and have been for quite some time—but these circumstances are anything but normal.

"I guess I'll have to see him for myself to be sure," Emma says with a wink and I groan.

"Can I just order some foo—oh, crap." No, no, no.

"What?" Emma stands upright and follows my gaze to the front door where none other than Mr. Pain in My Ass just stepped inside. "Damn," she mutters. "That's him, huh?"

This day can't possibly get any worse. "Yes, that's him," I grumble, keeping my eyes on my drink and wishing I could absorb right into this stool. I doubt he'll come over if he sees me, but I don't want to take any chances. We may be neighbors, but I'm not feeling particularly neighborly about it.

"Al, he's gorgeous," my brother's fiancée rasps out the side of her mouth. "And I hate to be the bearer of bad news, but he's not only looking at you, he's also coming over, too."

Dammit. The whole point of coming out tonight was to hash this whole thing out with Emma, but I can't very well do it with him here, now can I?

"Howdy, neighbor," he says when he sidles up next to the empty stool beside me, his voice low and smooth and friendly, as if I wasn't rude when we met earlier. "Mind if I join you?"

I absolutely mind. In fact, I'm not even hungry anymore. I should just go—

"Of course, she doesn't!" Emma slams her hand down on the bar with such gusto that I jump. "Right, Al? In fact, I was just about to take her order and hook her up with dinner for the night. Can I get you something while I'm at it?"

"That's what I'm here for," he says, grinning and dropping his denim-clad butt down onto the stool. "You said something earlier about having the best cheeseburgers in town, and I've been thinking about 'em ever since."

Wait, what?

I pin Emma with a hard glare and she merely presses her lips into a smile and retreats backward toward the kitchen, knowing damn well she's in trouble.

"You want a double cheeseburger?" she asks Holden. "Fries, onion rings, mozzarella sticks, or maybe some deep fried pickles?"

"Surprise me." He winks and a low chuckle vibrates the air around him as he leans his elbows on the bar.

Emma is barely out of earshot before I spin to face him. "You saw Emma already?"

"Yeah, when I met Aiden here earlier. Why?"

I'm going to kill her. She didn't hear about him through the grapevine—she knew firsthand. Which means she also knew about him rooming across the hall from me, too. And she never gave me a heads-up either.

What the heck is wrong with everyone?

"Listen," he says, angling toward me so it's hard to miss the genuine sparkle in his eyes. "I think we've gotten off on the wrong foot here."

"You think?"

He gives a small smile. "I understand why you'd feel put

out or even pissed off about the whole bathroom thing. You don't know me. I don't know you. It's weird. But we're kind of stuck in the situation. All we can do at this point is make the best of it."

"Or you could find someplace else to stay." Wow, I sound like a bitch. I almost don't even recognize my own voice or this bitterness running through my veins.

"Afraid I can't do that, darlin'." He winks and a shiver runs down my spine.

"Darlin'?" I ask, suddenly a little breathless. Obviously, it's a side effect of him taking up so damn much space and crowding me.

His gaze locks on mine and he smiles. "Yep, and I hope you don't mind me saying, but I do believe you have the prettiest set of hazel eyes I've ever seen."

"It's Alana. And clearly you don't get out much."

He laughs again and shakes his head. "I get out plenty. Then again maybe it's not the color of your eyes I'm drawn to but the fire behind them."

Drawn to? Is this guy flirting with me? I know I'm out of practice, but either he's flirting or he's trying to butter me up in hopes I'll share my shampoo and towels.

"Why exactly are you here?" I ask bluntly. "In Mason Creek, I mean."

He lifts a shoulder. "Wilder needed some help on the ranch and I happened to be laid off for a bit."

"What do you do for a living?"

"I work with livestock mostly."

"Like a ranch hand?"

He twists his lips and nods. "You could say that."

Hmm. "Why are you laid off?"

"Damn, darlin'." He chuckles. "Why so many questions?"

"Because there's going to be nothing but two doors and a

hallway separating us. I'd like to know you're not a serial killer."

He tips his head back and gives a full-bellied laugh as Emma comes back from the kitchen.

"Can I get you something to drink?" she asks him, not even bothering to look my way, because she knows better. This girl and I are going to have a serious talk about this as soon as possible.

"I'll take a bottle of Coors."

"I have Light or Banquet."

"Banquet would be great."

"Coming up." She spins away and begins taking another order while grabbing his beer.

Holden uses the opportunity to continue talking. "My boss asked me to take a voluntary leave for a few weeks. Had some stuff to deal with."

Oh. Well, that doesn't sound as scandalous as I was antici-pating. "How do you know Wilder?"

"A friend of a guy I work with."

"And my brother?"

"Same. We met a few times over the years and, when the opportunity presented itself, I figured they seemed like decent enough guys to work with."

"My brother is a cop, not a rancher."

"I know, but he helped hook me up." He smirks and shakes his head. "Are you always this tough of a nut to crack or is this skepticism and game of Twenty Questions just for me?"

"I like to know who's using my toothpaste."

"I have my own stuff, Alana. I'm not here to mooch off you."

Hmm. "Night owl or morning person?"

"What?" He laughs and swaps some cash for the beer

Emma sets in front of him. "What does that have to do with anything?"

"I'm usually up late doing homework, so I like it quiet."

"Me too. I outgrew partying years ago. In fact, this is the first bar I've been to in months."

I hope he's telling the truth. As annoying as the bathroom predicament is, it'd be even worse if he was loud.

"What are you going to school for?"

"Business management."

"You manage the grocery store, right?" He tips back his beer and glances my way, dark chocolate eyes darting back and forth between mine.

I swallow and nod, suddenly self-conscious about that fact, which isn't something I've felt in years. I used to struggle with feeling like I'd given up on my dreams, and for some reason, I don't want this guy—a virtual stranger—to think it's because I lack ambition for more.

"That's cool," he says. "From what Aiden said, the place would fall apart without you. You must be really good at what you do."

My brother said that? Wow. Aiden and I aren't as close as we used to be, because he'd been living in L.A. for so long. But now that he's back in Mason Creek, our relationship is changing. He's still a pain in my ass, just a slightly more lovable pain in the ass.

"I like to think I do a good job. We've turned a bigger profit since I took over, but we've managed to keep our prices low so the locals don't feel like they have to go to the box stores in Billings to afford their groceries."

"That's really important in small towns like this."

"Yeah? You know a little something about small-town living?"

"Yep. The one I live in is pretty much the same size. The

only thing we have going for us is a big music festival every year."

"Where is this mystery place?"

"Bear Creek, Colorado."

"Really? I've been through Bear Creek a bunch of times. I have family in Boulder."

His eyes widen. "You serious?"

"Yep. My uncle is a pediatrician and my aunt is pretty much the chairwoman of every social club."

The grin on his face spreads wide, revealing a perfect set of white teeth amidst the light brown five o'clock shadow. "Small world."

"For sure." I sigh and take a sip of my Dr. Pepper.

"Not a drinker?"

I shrug. "It's not that I don't, I just don't do it often. School and work have kept me busy." And when the heck did I stop hating this guy and started having an actual conversation with him?

"Did you walk here tonight?"

"Yup. I like the fresh air."

"Me, too." He glances around the bar filled with patrons either minding their own business or chatting politely with other customers. Even the college-aged guys at the pool tables are behaving themselves. "Nice little town y'all have here. A girl like you probably doesn't have much to worry about, walking around town alone at night."

"A girl like me?" I pull back, brows lifted. "What exactly does that mean?" I know he's not insinuating that I couldn't take care of myself…

He grins and his eyes crinkle a bit. "Simmer down, darlin'. I have no doubt you could kick someone's ass if they even thought about messing with you."

"You're damn right I could." I mean, probably. And I could get used to this *darlin'* business.

He chuckles again, running his thumb up and down the side of his bottle of beer. "Speaking of kicking ass, you got a boyfriend I should be worried about? Someone who might see me keeping you company and get pissed?"

"And if I did?"

He smirks like he's already made the assumption I'm single and something about that irritates me.

"Maybe I have a girlfriend."

His brows lift. "Do you?"

As much as I want to continue the ruse just to yank his chain, I really don't want to keep talking about the sad state of my love life. "No," I sigh.

"Thank god."

This time, it's my brows that rise. "Excuse me?"

"I thought I read you all wrong for a second. That you were into chicks instead of dudes."

Well, that's interesting. "I tried that. I mean, in theory anyway. I didn't get very far."

"I feel like there's a story here."

"There is, but I don't talk about it. Suffice to say, I've given up on men."

His expression falls. "Shit. That's more tragic than you being into women."

I laugh. "Blame it on the Megatron of asshole exes."

"Must have been a real piece of work to make you consider switching teams."

"Not just a piece... he was the whole freaking gallery."

"Damn."

"Uh huh."

"So the stick your brother said you have up your ass... it's justified."

I snort so hard soda nearly comes out my nose. "I'm going to kill him."

"I'm kidding." He prods me with an elbow. "Just trying to

make light of things. Hoping to somehow get on your good side."

I figured as much. "Listen, I'm only tolerating this conversation because I know at any moment, Emma is going to bring me delish food that's going to make me forget about all of this. I'm still not happy about you poaching my space." And maybe because he's mildly interesting. And majorly cute.

He grins. "You know what? I'll take it. And I'm going to make it my personal mission to make you actually want to talk to me by the time I leave."

"Don't be too tough on yourself when you don't succeed. I'm kinda known as the Ice Princess around here."

"Oh really?" He smirks as one of the waitresses comes from the kitchen with two baskets of food. She sets the one with extra fries in front of me and the one with onion rings and a mountain of meat in front of Holden. After she grabs the ketchup and mustard and a stack of napkins, she disappears again. "Why do they call you the Ice Princess?"

"It's more of a general perception than a nickname." All because of a certain bull rider who liked to ride more than just the bulls.

Holden eyes me for a long beat. So long that I squirm in my seat.

"Why are you looking at me like that?"

His jaw pulses as he swallows. "Just trying to figure you out, darlin', that's all."

"Well, don't try too hard, because you're not going to be here long enough to make it worth your while."

A small smirk turns up the corners of his mouth and those brown eyes twinkle beneath the bar lights. "Something you should know about me is that I love a challenge and you, darlin', are a puzzle I am determined to figure out."

# CHAPTER 3

HOLDEN

*B*y the time noon rolls around on Thursday, I'm dragging ass.

I work about half of the year at my uncle's ranch in Colorado, but I've been off for the past few months, traveling from city to city on the summer rodeo trail. I still train damn near every day, but nothing compares to the physical labor of working a ranch.

"Break time," Wilder announces, hopping out of the tractor and tossing his gloves onto the back fender. He swipes the back of his hand across his forehead beaded with sweat. We've been drilling new fence post holes for the last four hours and, right now, the hot August sun is at its peak.

"Thank god," I mutter, immediately going for a bottle of water in the cooler I stowed in the back of the ranch truck. "Not to sound like a pussy, but I might be too out of shape for this."

Wilder snorts. "That's the difference between you show-boaters and us real cowboys."

"Yeah, yeah." He's not wrong, but I'm not about to admit it. "Just give me a couple days and I'll be running laps around your ass."

"Sure you will." He chuckles and hops up onto the tailgate of the truck, situating himself in front of the remaining fence posts.

Cracking open a water, I lean against the box. "Thanks again for this, man. I appreciate you keeping me busy while this shitstorm blows over. I could have gone back to my uncle's place, but I'd rather my family not get dragged into this mess."

He dips his chin. "No problem. I'm benefiting from it, too. You hear anything about what's going on? Any progress?"

"Not a thing. At this point, I'm not really expecting to, either." CJ, my manager, more or less told me to suck it up and take my lashings even though I had nothing to do with the latest drama. I'd already left town after the Tulsa ride. There was no way I could have been at the bar where I'd been accused of sexually assaulting a barely legal college girl. Yet that's what happened. She went to the cops, told them it was an ABR rider, and picked out my picture out of the lineup from the event.

Thankfully, I had gas and toll receipts to prove I was already on my way back to Colorado. But since the accuser came from a well-off, well-known family in the city, her accusation still spread like wildfire. The cops reviewed the toll cameras in Kansas, verified it was me driving my truck, and let me go. And in four to six months, the sexual assault kit test will double prove my innocence. But it didn't matter. The ABR still suspended my membership and thus my ability to ride.

CJ said this forced hiatus is for my own good, but I know it's less about me and more about saving the reputation of the ABR. The more the media camps outside of my house or the venues, trying to figure out which one of us fucked up, the more money the organization has to invest in mitigation. I'm a liability right now and, if I'm honest, it's a slap in the damn face. I could have placed in the top three this year. I've ridden twenty-four bulls and was fifth in points overall. And it didn't matter.

"Still think it's pretty shitty they aren't supporting you through this. That they're acting like you're guilty despite the evidence saying you're not."

"You're telling me," I mutter. "CJ said a month away should be enough to let things simmer down so I can be reinstated, but I don't see how it's going to matter." My reputation is pretty much screwed if the ABR won't support me.

"You never know. Something could happen between now and then that works to your benefit. Maybe this girl identifies the real asshole or, as much as I hate to say it, maybe he strikes again and is caught."

I nod and slam down the rest of my water. "I sure hope something gives, because I just want to get back to doing what I love."

"Well if there's anything more I can do to help, let me know."

"I appreciate that."

"I'm real sorry about the cabins being unavailable, too. I know that little room Old Man Morton has to offer isn't much. Aiden said it's at least partly furnished?"

"Yeah, it's not the worst setup in the world. I've definitely slept in shadier accommodations over the years, and it's nice being in town so I can grab dinner since there's not a stove or anything."

"You meet Alana yet?"

Her whiskey eyes flash through my mind and I smile. "Yep. Ended up sharing dinner with her at Pony Up last night. Seems nice." Once I broke through that first icy layer, anyway.

Wilder smirks. "You know who she is, right?"

I nod. "Aiden told me." It doesn't matter that she's his sister, though, because I don't plan on being here long enough to be more than her neighbor. Even if she is the prettiest damn thing I've seen in a while.

"She's so friggin' smart and she's busted her ass to pay for school. Owning a farm, her folks really never had the money to help her out. She was lucky enough to land a softball scholarship, but once everything went down and she left Montana State, she lost it all."

I'd love to know what "everything" is he's referring to, but it's not really my business, so I don't ask.

"Anyway, if she comes off a little guarded, that's why. She's one of the sweetest people I know, but it may take some time for her to warm up to you. Once you thaw her a bit, you'll love her as much as we do."

"Good to know." Seems like the least I can do is keep trying to be friendly with her seeing as she's opened up her private space to me, albeit begrudgingly.

"Oh, shoot, I forgot to mention—Hallie said you're welcome to join us for dinner while you're here, so you don't have to eat in town every night."

I grin and toss my empty water bottle into my cooler. I've traveled all over the country, but in the day I've been here, Mason Creek is already shaping up to be one of the friendliest towns I've had the pleasure of visiting.

"Thanks," I tell him, dipping my chin. "That's awfully kind of her. Tell her I might take her up on the offer a time or two. I don't want to make this a three's-a-crowd situation, though, and intrude on you and your woman. I'm sure you have better things to do than entertain me." I lift an eyebrow, and he chuckles.

"I can suck it up every now and then, but since I've only recently secured this relationship myself, I'd kinda like to enjoy the honeymoon period a bit more, ya know?"

I do. Even though it's been a while since I've been in a serious relationship, I remember those early days fondly despite the bitter endings that always followed.

"Speaking of my woman, I'm going to call her and check in, then we'll get back to the fence. Hopefully we can get it done before Levi and Caleb get back, so we can give them shit for not helping."

I laugh. "Sounds like my kind of fun."

I met Levi and Caleb yesterday, but they were already headed to Billings with a couple of cattle for butchering when I arrived at the Roman Wilde Ranch just before five thirty this morning.

It's obvious Wilder and his crew are made for this kind of work and their commitment is admirable. If I'm honest, I'm a little envious they get to do this year-round. I've worked part time on my uncle's ranch in Colorado since I was a kid, and while the work isn't for the faint of heart, there's a hell of a lot of gratification in knowing you gave it your all and got it done.

Bull riding is similar. In fact, I firmly believe that if you're gonna get on an animal and not give it your all, you have no fucking business getting on in the first place.

But bull riding is also a game. Sure, the prizes are nice, and the buckles and the payouts and the notoriety are amazing for my ego. But they aren't the same kind of reward as knowing you busted your ass from sunup until sundown. That's a whole other kind of gratification, and having the opportunity to feel that again for a little while is the only damn reason I agreed to come to Mason Creek in the first place.

"Hallie said she's making extra chicken alfredo for dinner

tonight, so you'd better show up," Wilder says as he returns with his phone in hand.

"Is that so?" I chuckle and finish off my bag of almonds. "I guess I could do that."

He smirks as he adjusts his hat and tips his head toward the fence. "Smart man. Now let's get back to work."

ALANA

"I heard you have a new neighbor."

Tucking the daily bank deposit slip into the bag and quickly thanking the teller for her help, I turn to find Hallie standing behind me with a mischievous grin on her face. Her blonde hair is twisted up into a bun, and she's dressed in a pretty blue pantsuit that makes her look all prim and proper and nothing at all like the jeans and T-shirt girl who used to work at the butcher shop.

"Hey, Ms. Financial Advisor. How's the new job going?" I push a loose strand of hair behind my ear, suddenly feeling underdressed and disheveled in my jeans, tank top, and Converse shoes.

"It's great!" she chirps, clasping her hands in front of herself and bouncing a little on her toes. "So, what do you think of Holden? I assume you've met him already, right?"

Dang it, I thought maybe if I ignored her first question, she'd forget she asked.

"Oh, right. Holden. Yeah, he seems okay. He said he's working at the ranch with Wilder and Levi?"

"Uh huh. It'll be nice to have an extra set of hands for a while. Maybe it'll even give me a little more time with my man." She waggles her eyebrows and I laugh quietly.

29

"Well, I hope that's the case." I don't spend as much time with my friends as I'd like, but of course I want them all to be happy. Just because my love life is crap doesn't mean I wish theirs to be.

"Me, too." She waves at her boss, Brayden, as he walks by and then out the side of her mouth mutters, "I should probably get back to work, but if I recall correctly, you promised you'd come over for dinner and visit the last time we saw each other."

Ah. Yep. Yep, I sure did. "I'm sorry. I've been so busy with the store and then I had summer classes…"

She presses her lips together in a knowing smirk. "Girl, you have to start taking some time for yourself. You know, enjoy life a little. Socialize. Have fun."

Ugh. In theory, sure. In reality, there simply aren't enough hours in the day. Maybe in the spring when I'm finally done with school.

"Come over tonight," she continues, taking a step forward and lowering her voice a bit. "Please, Alana. I hate knowing how hard you're working without any reprieve. Let me at least feed you."

I open my mouth to decline her offer as politely as possible, but she beats me to the punch.

"I won't take no for an answer, so don't even think about it. Besides, I'm making homemade alfredo and it's pretty much to die for."

Dang it, I love alfredo. "You run a hard bargain, Hal."

She wrinkles up her nose and begins to retreat back toward her office. "Come by at six o'clock."

"Should I bring anything?"

"Just your perky self." She gives a little finger wave before spinning on her heels and getting back to work.

I do the same, trying to be as perky as possible, as I return to the Mason Creek Market just in time to see the wave of water sluice from beneath the door of the women's bath-room, across the black and white tiled floor, and all the way to the service desk.

"Alana!" Susie shrieks when she sees me and I sigh.

Something tells me Hallie's invitation couldn't have come at a better time. When I'm done with this mess, I'm not going to want to do anything but sit back and relax.

# CHAPTER 4

HOLDEN

"*H*old up, I thought you were staying for dinner!" Wilder calls as I head for my truck after we finally call it quits for the day.

"Dude, I need a shower." Providing, of course, my gorgeous neighbor hasn't locked me out of the bathroom again like she did this morning, forgetting our arrangement.

"Oh, okay." Wilder strolls over at a fast clip while digging out his wallet. "Do me a favor and grab a six-pack of Coors from the store while you're there, too, will ya?" He hands over the cash and I nod.

"Sure thing."

"Thanks, man. See you again in a few." He heads back to his truck and I climb into mine, quickly checking my phone. Normally, I'm attached at the hip to the damn thing, but today I left it charging in the truck, mostly because I didn't want to deal with the circuit drama. One glance at the screen says I made the right call. Nine missed calls from CJ and a dozen texts from my buddies on the circuit, minus Cory, despite it being his idea I come up to Montana.

I scan the messages with a sigh and see that they're mostly about whether or not I've heard anything new about returning. CJ's, however, is a pointed, *Answer your damn phone, Mack*.

Grumbling, I hit his contact and put the phone on speaker as I start the truck and head toward town.

"About friggin' time," he barks, and I tighten my hands around the steering wheel.

"I was at work," I snap back. "You know, since I don't have another gig at the moment. Unless you're calling to tell me something has changed."

He makes a throaty sound. "You know it hasn't."

"Then what do you want?" Because I had a good day today and I sure as hell don't need him ruining that.

"One of the video girls was assaulted after our ride last weekend in Omaha. She got away before he could finish, but she was pretty beat up."

"Ah, shit." I run a hand around the back of my neck as the blood coursing through my veins seems to chill and boil at the same time. Thank god, they can't try and pin this on me, but I hate that someone else got hurt. "Which girl?" I grit out.

"Victoria."

*Goddammit.* I slow the truck at an intersection and close my eyes as Vickie's face flashes through my mind. I know her well enough that her baby blues and blonde hair come easy. She's recorded my rides for the past two seasons and I took her out a few times as thanks.

"She okay?" I ask, my gut clenching.

"Yeah." CJ clears his throat. "She's fine. She already told the cops she's one-hundred-percent sure it wasn't you."

Yeah, no shit. I've been hundreds of miles away for days now and the fact that I was even mentioned pisses me off.

"Anyway, I just wanted you to know," CJ adds.

"Thanks. Does this mean I can come back?"

He doesn't answer right away and the ache in my stomach turns to lead. Why the hell am I being punished for something I didn't do? And why the hell aren't the people who allegedly have my best interest at heart doing anything to help me?

"Nah, Mack, you know the plan. We have to stick to it."

"This is such bullshit!" I snap as a vehicle behind me honks and I remember I'm at a stop sign. I hit the gas and crank my truck toward town. "They know it's not me. Hell, they knew the day after the first attack it wasn't, but here I am, cast away to the middle of Nowhere, Montana like a fucking criminal."

"It's for your own good, Mack. We've been over this. The ABR is trying to protect you from the media and the press."

"Oh, really?" I give a bitter laugh. "Then why don't they say that? Why don't they tell the press I'm innocent and that this time-out isn't because they think otherwise?"

He's quiet again and I don't bother waiting for an answer.

"I gotta go. Don't call me again unless it's to tell me the ABR has pulled their head from their ass." I click off the phone and toss it into the passenger seat.

I rehash the bullshit that's become my life all the way to the red brick building I'm temporarily calling home. The Mason Creek Market is still open and I pray like hell Alana's working so I won't have to worry about any awkward bathroom run-ins, especially since I'm in a rush. I need to get back to the ranch before I piss off Hallie.

I hop out of the truck and jog to the back door. Reaching for the handle, I'm almost clocked in the head when it flies open and my gorgeous neighbor rushes out.

"Whoa!" My hands go to her shoulders. The jolt of shock quickly replaced with the fact that her shoulders are bare and, despite the fact that I'm holding her, her skin feels like it's branding *me*. And yet I don't let go. "Slow down, darlin'," I tell her, as we stand there, both of us breathing fast as we stare at each other.

This close, I realize she's not quite as tall as I thought she was. Shit, she barely comes to my chin.

"Can you please let go of me?" she asks by way of greeting. "I'm running late."

"Hot date?" I tease, though I don't have a second to spare on this kind of playful small talk.

"Yep." She gives her head a solitary nod and something almost spiteful flashes in her amber eyes.

"I thought you didn't have a boyfriend." I wink and she rolls her eyes.

"I have to get going or I'll be late."

"Don't let me stop you, darlin'." I step aside and she rushes past, the scent of cherry and something sugary tickling my nose in her wake. "You want me to leave the light on or anything?" I call after her. "You got protection?"

She raises her arm in the air and gives me a single finger salute before sliding behind the wheel of her Camry.

All I can do is laugh… and anticipate our next run-in.

ALANA

"Ah, you're really here! And you brought wine!" Hallie exclaims as she opens the front door to the home she now shares with Wilder. I've been out here a few times over the years since Wilder built the cabin, along with the smaller cabins he usually has available for rent, so the changes in the place since Hallie moved in are obvious. From the flowerpots on the front porch to the welcome mat to the rich, mouthwatering aroma of creamy garlic wafting through the air, this is now Hallie's home just as much as it is his.

"Of course, I am." I laugh, letting her pull me in for a quick hug before I follow her inside and set the wine on the kitchen counter while she returns to the stove. "And I couldn't very well come empty-handed."

"I will never turn down a glass of wine." She tosses a wink over her shoulder, then nods to the cupboard. "Glasses are up there if you want to do the honors."

I smile and make quick work of pulling out a long-stemmed glass for each of us. I won't drink more than this single glass since I have to drive back into town, but after the day I've had, I am more than ready to slow down and enjoy this delicious sweetness.

"Is Wilder still working?" I ask as I uncork the bottle. "I didn't see his truck out front."

"He had to run back to the main house to drop some paperwork off for Levi. He should be back any minute. He was pretty excited to hear you were coming tonight. He said he hasn't really seen you since Madelyn was home last."

I laugh. "Yes, it's been a while since I harassed him. Tonight should be fun." Wilder and Levi's baby sister has been my best friend for as long as I can remember, so, by association, the guys have always been like big brothers to me, too. We don't see each other very often because our work keeps us busy, but we have the kind of friendship that falls right back into place, no matter how much time goes by between visits.

"Fun indeed." Hallie glances back with another smile. "So, how are things at the market?"

"Ugh." Taking my wine, I claim a chair at the table. "Other than the volcanic eruption that came from the toilet in the women's bathroom this afternoon, things have been good."

"Oh, gosh, do I even want to know?" She grimaces as she stirs what I assume is the alfredo sauce.

"No. It was a mess. Thankfully, Sadie's dad got there fast and all I had to do was mop it up."

"As if that's not bad enough."

No kidding. But I'm not going to complain about it, because doing so feels like I'm just asking for bad juju. If I want to eventually own the place, not just run it, I can't invite that kind of negativity into my head.

"Marty was in the bank the other day talking with Brayden. I might've overheard him talking about putting the store up for sale at some point."

Gulping down my immediate response—again, no negativity allowed—I paste on a smile. "He's been talking about it for years, though I think he's actually serious now."

Hallie nods. "I can see that. He's not getting any younger."

"Nope, he sure isn't." I sip my wine and sigh. "I know you're technically off the clock, but do you mind if I ask you a few financial questions?"

She glances back with a raised eyebrow. "Not at all. What's on your mind?"

"Well…" I've never really talked with anyone about this beyond using it as a hypothetical situation in a couple of my business classes, but if Old Man Morton is getting serious about selling, I have to get serious about my game plan, too. "I haven't told anyone, but I'd love to buy the place myself."

Hallie's eyes go wide over a grin. "Really? I mean, I'm not surprised. You already do everything but sign the checks."

"Yeah." With another sigh, I swirl the golden liquid around in my glass. "I've already worked on a draft business plan, but the problem is I haven't been able to save as much as I'd hoped because of tuition." Changing majors from public relations to business when I finally returned to college meant I had to retake an entire year of credits. And having essentially dropped out after the breakup with Cory, I lost my scholarship. I've been eligible for a small amount of financial aid, but being single, I make too much money to qualify for anything significant. I'm stuck in that dreaded middle of not being poor, but not being well-off, either.

"Right. That's a tough position to be in. You know, there are some programs that offer grants for start-up costs. Or maybe Marty would be open to lease the store to you until you can afford to buy it outright."

I've researched the grant programs and even reached out to speak with one of the coordinators. The thing is I need to know for sure that I'm going to buy the place before I can apply. I need documentation from a bank and even from Marty to prove my intentions are legit. That's where I get nervous, because I'm not sure if I could secure a loan. I have great credit, but that damn lack of capital…

"Is there any way to find out if I qualify for a loan? And what I would need for a down payment?"

"For sure!" Hallie says eagerly. "Call me tomorrow when I'm in front of my calendar and we'll set up a time to sit down and crunch numbers."

A modicum of relief settles into my shoulders. By no means is a simple conversation going to seal the deal, but it's a step in the right direction. A step I've been hesitant to take based solely on the fear of being rejected. Thanks a freaking lot, Cory Mitchell.

Suddenly, there's a knock on the front door and Hallie and I both jump at the same time.

"Oh, shoot, I almost forgot…" Hallie presses her hand over her heart at the same time a timer goes off on the stove and she jumps again. "Shoot! Can you grab the door while I get the bread out of the oven?"

"Sure thing." I set my wine down and pad to the front of

the house, opening the door without bothering to ask who she's expecting.

"Well, well," Holden chides from the porch with a smirk. "This is your hot date, huh?" he taunts, his gaze slowly sliding down my body and back up again as I cross my arms over my chest. I don't know what it is about this guy, but for some reason, my girls really seem to like him. Especially when he does that whole head-to-toe sweep he likes to do. Unfortunately for him, there's not much to see. I'm wearing jeans and a plain white tank top, which sorta matches the jeans and snug white tee he's wearing.

"Are you lost?" I ask with a put-on smile. If it were my door he'd knocked at, I probably would have shut it in his face but this is Wilder and Hallie's place, not mine.

"Nope, I don't believe I am." He makes a show of checking his watch, which draws my attention to his arms. His thick, tanned, delicious arms. "I have a dinner invitation for exactly this time."

A dinner invitation? Dammit, Hallie.

His grin hitches to one side as he tucks his hands into his pockets and rocks back on the heels of his boots. "Let me guess—they invited you, too, and forgot to mention I was coming."

"Actually, I think the lack of communication was probably more to protect you than me, considering you're somewhat of a charity case, are you not, Mr...." Crap, I don't even know his last name.

One eyebrow lifts and I swear fire flashes in his eyes even though he's still smirking. "McMurray," he says in a low, confident tone. "But you don't need to be formal on my account. I mean, we do share a bathroom, which is practically like sharing a bedroom."

A shiver runs from the base of my neck all the way down to my tailbone at his saucy tone and that taunting gleam in his eyes. I want to say it was the bad kind of shiver, but that little zap has the blood rushing from my already aroused nipples straight to the center of my legs, too.

Then again, maybe that's the worst kind of shiver where Holden McMurray, invader of my privacy, is concerned.

"You're something else," I mutter, narrowing my eyes and shaking my head, which he apparently finds funny, given his full-bellied laugh.

"Oh, Alana, you keep saying that like it's a bad thing…" He shuffles closer, so close in fact that I can smell the clean, citrusy scent of soap or body wash wafting off of him. He must have bought his own, because he definitely doesn't smell like my cherry vanilla. "But I'm starting to think your disgust is all for show, because what you're trying to hide behind those folded arms…" His eyes fall to my chest and he bites his lip, his face just inches from mine. "It tells me something very different."

I hate him. I absolutely freaking hate him. "You know what? I'm suddenly not hungry anymore. I'm going home."

"What?" Out of nowhere, Wilder appears, a deep crease in his brow. "Why are you leaving? Because of this guy?" He claps Holden on the back. "What the hell did you do to piss her off now?"

Holden chuckles as he stands upright again and I want to slap the smug grin right off his ridiculously handsome face. Seriously, who needs a chiseled jaw like that? Or those sexy, smoldering eyes?

"Apparently, I took a breath," he says. "Gotta admit it's been a while since that's all it took for a woman to despise me like she does."

Wilder shakes with laughter. "Hate to break it to you, man, but if she's not happy with you, it's probably your fault. She may come off chilly because she's so damn busy and doesn't have time for bullshit, but she's not the spiteful type."

Uh huh. And come to think of it, I should be pissed at Wilder just the same, because he's the one who brought this guy here without having another place for him to stay.

Since I lied about not being hungry and I'd kind of like to eat Hallie's homemade chicken alfredo, I suck it up and keep my mouth shut.

I'm not happy with Wilder, either, but I'll keep my beef contained to the lighter haired of the tall, too-good-looking-for-their-own-good men standing before me.

# CHAPTER 5

HOLDEN

*A*nd here I thought I made progress with Alana last night at Pony Up. Hell, she'd even laughed a little, not to mention smiled toward the end of our conversation and when we'd parted ways at her door.

Then again, it was no secret she wasn't happy about me invading her privacy, and now here I am, poaching on her time with her friends, too.

I should feel bad. And maybe a small part of me does. But I've been around enough women in my twenty-seven years to know well and good that she's just as intrigued as she is spiteful. And that's all I need to know.

"So, how was your first day on the ranch?" Hallie asks after we've passed around the serving dishes and loaded our plates.

I clear my throat. "Great. Felt good to put in a full day's work again." I almost admit that it's been a while since I've done actual ranch work, but stop short when I remember I'm supposed to keep that tidbit of info to myself. Of course,

Wilder knows the truth, but the last thing I need is Alana knowing about my drama and disapproving of me even more than she already does.

"He's a little rusty," Wilder says with a grin from across the table. "But we'll get him operating a full bore again in no time."

"Rusty?" Alana speaks up from the chair beside me and when I glance her way, one eyebrow is arched curiously.

Dammit, Wilder.

"I told you I was laid off, right?" I ask in what I hope is a pleasant, believable tone. After all, it's not really a lie. It's just not the whole truth, either.

She presses her lips together and nods, the suspicion in her expression easing a bit.

"All in all, it was a good day, though. Gonna be a little sore tomorrow, but it won't be anything a hot shower can't take care of."

Alana snorts and Hallie glances back and forth between the two of us like she's just waiting for something to go down. But, as tempted as I am to goad my pretty new neighbor about our situation, I won't. Not in front of our friends, who were kind enough to invite us both into their home and offer us this amazing food.

We spend the next forty-five minutes making small talk and eating what is, hands down, the best meal I've eaten in weeks. When we're finished, Hallie and Alana clean up, and Wilder invites me to the front porch for a beer.

"Nice night," I say, lowering into a lawn chair as the sun sets down behind the mountains in the distance. "Thanks for the invitation, by the way."

"All Hallie." Wilder lifts his hands, one of them wrapped around a bottle of Coors. "Same with Alana. I had no idea she was coming and I get the impression you probably would have appreciated a heads-up about that."

I grin. "Nah, it's all good. Obviously, she isn't thrilled with our situation, but I can't say I blame her."

"Thought you had dinner with her last night." He cocks an eyebrow.

"More like I stumbled into Pony Up and forced my company on her, hoping if she got to know me a little, she'd be less skeptical. I thought it'd worked, but I guess not."

Wilder sniffs and kicks back a bit in his seat, crossing one ankle over the other. "She'll come around. She might not fall in love with ya or anything, all things considered, but she'll warm up eventually."

I snort as I bring my beer to my lips. "Yeah, I'm not looking for love, so we're good on that front."

He flashes me a sidelong smirk. "She's pretty, though, right?"

An instantaneous image of her standing beneath the spray of the shower zips through my mind and my dick twitches. I may or may not have lain in bed last night, listening to the shower and guessing what she'd look like if I snuck in and peeked behind the curtain. I'd never, of course, but that didn't stop me from imagining her long dark hair and those luscious curves, all soaked and sudsed up.

"Yeah, she's pretty," I agree, dropping my voice so she can't hear me from in the house. "I know it's not my business, but what's the story with her, anyway?"

He cocks his head to the side. "I thought Aiden told you."

"A little, but something tells me there's more to it."

"You could say that." Wilder cranes his head from side to side and stares off toward the sunset, like he's trying to decide whether or not he should be the one to spill Alana's secrets. He sucks in a breath and opens his mouth just as the screen door creaks and the ladies stroll out.

"Oh, the sunset is gorgeous!" Hallie gasps, taking a seat on

Wilder's lap with her gaze cast toward the orange and purple streaked sky in the distance.

Alana leans over the porch railing with a sigh. "I swear you guys have the best view in Mason Creek."

With her back to me, my eyes fall to her ass encased in those snug jeans. At the moment, I'm pretty sure I'm the one with the best view in Mason Creek, but I keep that to myself.

"I should probably get going," she says, turning back to us. "The fall semester just started this week and I want to get a head start."

"Al, you work every weekend. In fact, you work every day of the week." Hallie's tone is almost big sisterlike. Concerned. Just like the crease in her brow. "How haven't you burned out yet?"

Alana's cheeks flush a bit as she stubs the toe of her Converse sneaker into the porch floor. "I'm fine. Besides, it's not like working at a grocery store is hard work."

If all she did all day was bag groceries, maybe not. But from what I understand, she does it all. Ordering, inventory, employee issues, etc. That's a hell of a lot for one person.

"I've been thinking about planning a girls' weekend with Emma and Madelyn," Hallie says. "I'd really like you to come. Do you think Marty would give you a few days off?"

Alana bites her lip and shrugs. "Maybe. I mean, fall sports are starting up for the kids and they're going to need time off for games and whatnot once school starts. It'd have to be soon. Before the rodeo, too."

Hallie's eyes light up. "I'll talk to the other girls and we'll get something pinned down."

Alana nods, but I'm not buying her agreement. In fact, it strikes me as odd that she's not jumping at the chance to hang out with her girls, especially if this girls' weekend is anything like the ones my sister has with her friends. Shopping, the spa, sangria, sunshine…

"Just let me know," she says, pasting on a smile that doesn't quite meet those gorgeous eyes. "Thank you so much for dinner. It was amazing and so much better than the Lean Cuisine I would have had otherwise."

Hallie peels herself away from Wilder and wraps Alana in a big hug that mimics the sisterly vibe from earlier. "I'll call you tomorrow after I talk with the other girls."

"Okay." Alana nods as they break apart, but before she can escape down the porch steps, Wilder pulls her close, too.

"Was good seeing you outside of the store, Alana Banana." When he lifts her off the porch in a bear hug, she giggles and swats at his back. "And if this guy here gives you any trouble, you know where to find me." He winks at me over her shoulder and I shake my head before tipping back a swig of beer.

"Oh, I'll be fine," she says as he sets her back down. "It's him you should be worried about."

"Is that so?" I laugh, pressing the back of my hand to my mouth to keep from choking. "You plan on giving me trouble?"

Her answer is a smart-ass smirk that's probably the most genuine I've seen from her yet. With a quick wave of her fingers and another round of goodbyes, she's in her car and backing out of the driveway.

Wilder watches after her for a beat before spinning around with a wide grin pinned square on me. Hallie's is similar.

"What?" I ask, looking between the both of them, puzzled.

Wilder just shakes his head, giving nothing away. "Nothing, man. Nothing at all."

Yeah, I don't believe that for a second, but I let it go, because something tells me I already know what he's thinking. I'm just not sure I'll be in Mason Creek long enough to prove him right.

ALANA

I'm in the middle of brushing my teeth when I hear foot-steps on the other side of the door between the bathroom and the hall. The heavy sound of boots on the creaky hard-wood floor pauses for a split second before the handle on the door jiggles, but doesn't open. Thankfully, I've always kept it locked, so doing so now is second nature. Remembering to unlock it, however, is another story.

"Just a second!" I call to Holden after I rinse off the tooth-brush and set it back in its holder. There are two holes in the cute little porcelain pineapple, but Holden keeps his tooth-brush in a light blue travel holder alongside his toothpaste. I'm not sure why, but knowing he's pretty much living out of a suitcase right now in a matchbox size room that was never meant for living quarters makes me feel guilty.

"No rush," he calls back. "I'll go and take my boots off while you finish up."

I haven't seen the inside of the room across the hall since Marty set it up for him, but I'm familiar enough with the old furniture Marty had in storage to imagine what Holden's space looks like. And the image isn't a pretty one. Definitely not the kind of place someone could stay in for more than a couple of days, but somehow Holden thinks he's going to make it work for a few weeks.

The least I can do is quit copping an attitude about the bathroom. Especially, since he doesn't seem like the creeper I expected him to be, even if he is one hell of a flirt.

Flipping the lock on the door, I pad back into my apart-ment, closing the middle door behind me as I go. Unfortu-nately, the lock is on the inside, so I can't lock it behind me and risk Holden forgetting to unlock it when he's done. Aside from me forgetting to unlock the door for him this morning, we haven't had any issues.

As I make my way back through my apartment, I flip off the kitchen light and then the lamp in the living room, heading straight to my room where my laptop is already open on the bed, waiting for me.

I changed into my pajamas as soon as I got home from Wilder and Hallie's, because I'd eaten so much that the button on my jeans was starting to hurt. My typical tank top and cotton shorts never felt better and, as I crawl onto the bed and adjust the pillows behind me and the headboard, I let out a grateful sigh.

I keep thinking about Hallie's invitation to spend some time with her, Mads, and the girls, and if I'm honest, it sounds like heaven. The thing is, I've never taken time away from the store in the four years I've worked there and I'm not sure now is the time to ask. I want Marty to know I'm committed to the store with every fiber of my being, so there's no doubt in his mind how badly I want the market when he finally decides to sell.

Then again, maybe now is the time to go, because if I do somehow figure out a way to buy the store, there's a very good chance I won't get another opportunity for a vacation in a very long time.

Sighing, I grab my laptop and get to work on the first of my two new classes. I'll think about the girls' trip once I'm up to speed here.

I finish reading through the syllabus when a noise in the living room snags my attention. It almost sounds like something hit the wall, but it happened so quickly that I can't be sure.

I don't move an inch as I listen carefully to see if it

happens again when movement in the living room beyond my open bedroom door stills my beating heart.

The bat swoops into my room a second later, going straight for my window and the curtains.

I scream. A blood-curdling, on my feet in a second, slamming the bedroom door behind me scream.

I don't stop running until I push open the bathroom door and slam it shut behind me, because if there's one thing I'm scared of it's bats. Bloodsucking, vampire-fanged bats.

Leaning against the door, I close my eyes and try to catch my breath... only then realizing that I'm not alone. My eyes spring open, falling promptly on the half-naked man standing in front of the mirror.

"Did you just scream?" Holden asks around a mouthful of toothpaste. Where I'm freaking the hell out, he's the picture of cool and calm and did I mention half naked in his jeans and nothing more?

"There's a bat in my bedroom," I pant, trying to look anywhere but at his broad chest and the dusting of golden brown hair covering it. "I am freaking terrified of bats."

He spits, rinses, and puts his toothbrush back in the travel holder. "I would have never guessed."

"This isn't funny."

"Afraid they might try to make you immortal?"

My gaze flicks to his. "Don't you dare give me shit about it."

He laughs. "I take it you're Team Jacob."

I glower. "Can you be serious right now, please?"

"Absolutely," he says, eyes sparkling as they drop from my face to my tank top. "I take rescuing damsels in distress very seriously, darlin'."

Just when I'd started to think he wasn't so bad...

"Holden, please," I beg, the adrenaline starting to subside and give way to fear. I don't know how I'm going to be able to sleep in my room tonight or do anything in my apartment for that matter, because if one could get in, then surely another could find its way inside, too.

He steps forward, his smirk softening a bit as his gaze sets on mine again. "I'll take care of it. Just breathe for me, okay?"

I nod and swallow hard before trying to do just that. But I can't seem to get enough air and my chest feels like it's weighed down by a pallet of canned goods.

"Hey…" His big hands lift to my upper arms, grasping me gently. "I got this."

I gulp again and rasp, "Okay."

His thumb strokes across my bare skin and goose bumps rise in its wake. "How do I get to your room?"

"The kitchen is on the other side of this door. The living room is to the right and then my room is in back to the left." I can feel his breath on my face, the minty scent tickling my nose and somehow calming me a bit. Or maybe it's the kind, protective look in his eyes. Or the way he's still touching me. "It went toward the window. I-I think it's in the curtains."

"I'm going to grab a towel." He gestures toward the stack on the shelf by the shower. "Broom?"

"In the closet in the kitchen."

He dips his chin, grabs a towel, and urges me away from the door before going in.

Less than five minutes later, he calls to me from inside my apartment. "I'm going to take it outside through your main door. Hold tight."

My heart still beats a mile a minute in my chest as I drop down onto the closed toilet, hanging my head in my hands.

At this point, I'm pretty much over the bat. The icky feeling coursing through my veins right now is straight-up humiliation. Not only did I almost pee my pants over a stupid freaking bat, I cowered like a baby in front of my new, incredibly hot and surprisingly kind neighbor whom I'm determined not to like.

I no longer have any reason to hate him. Not only is he neat and tidy in the bathroom we've been forced to share, he's proven to be good company on two occasions now, and he just saved me from having to convert my very comfortable bed into a coffin.

The bathroom door opens from the hallway a second later and Holden appears with an empty towel in hand.

"You should have killed it," I say quietly and he smiles.

"I didn't want to get blood all over your room and your towel." He used his foot to open the dirty clothes hamper and tosses the towel inside.

"I'm going to burn that," I mutter and he laughs, turning back to me with his hands on his hips. The motion draws my attention to his waist and the ridge upon ridge of exposed muscle.

"What would you have done if I wasn't here?"

"Called Marty or Aiden."

Another grin tips up one side of his mouth. "You come off like such a tough cookie, but you're really a softy, aren't you?"

I snort. "Everyone is afraid of something. Bats just happened to be my thing."

"I'm not just talking about the bat."

I glance up at him, frowning. "What do you mean?"

He tips his head toward my apartment. "Your room isn't what I expected."

Oh, crap. I hadn't really thought about him seeing my things when I'd begged him to save my life.

"Nothing to be embarrassed about." He takes a step forward and I push to my feet, quickly turning toward the middle door, suddenly aware that we've been hanging out in the bathroom, of all places.

"I'm not embarrassed, I just…" I don't like how jittery he makes me. Or how I'm keenly aware of him in a way I haven't been aware of a man in a long time. "I need to get back to my homework."

He continues to smile, like he's reading my thoughts and thoroughly enjoying it.

"Thank you for keeping me mortal."

He laughs and pushes a hand over his hair, the tension of the moment finally snapping. "No problem. Feel free to beckon my superhero services whenever you need."

A small smile curls at my own lips, because not only is he sweet and sexy, he's funny, too.

"Goodnight, Alana," he says behind me as I open the door.

"Goodnight, Holden."

## CHAPTER 6

HOLDEN

The alarm on my phone goes off at four o'clock in the morning, but I've been lying awake in this miserable twin bed for the last hour. I'd decided after night number one that I needed to grab one of those egg crate cushions, but ever since seeing Alana's bed, full of fluffy white bedding and a million pillows, all I can think about is how good it'd feel to crash into that.

Or maybe the real appeal of the bed is the woman who's currently sleeping in it. That's what occupied my mind for the past hour, my brain continually conjuring up the image of her lean, curvy body stretched out in nothing but that thin tank top and those itty-bitty shorts. Her long, dark hair spread out across her pillow. Those smoldering eyes blinking open to find mine on the pillow next to hers.

I didn't come to Mason Creek looking for a girl to spark my interest. Shit, I haven't even dated in over a year and even then I'm not sure what Vickie and I had going on was really dating. We sort of just fell together, bumping into each other when we were out on the road, sharing dinner here and there, and eventually our beds.

She was a great girl. Hell, she *is* a great girl. I hate what happened to her, but I'm not going to dig up her name in my contacts and reach out to see how she's doing.

I do, however, wish I had Alana's number so I could check in on her and not because it's the neighborly thing to do. No, my interest in her is something altogether different. It's something I haven't felt in a long time and, frankly, it's probably a good thing I don't have her number, because the very last thing I need is to get to know—and start liking—a girl I'm going to have to walk away from in a few weeks.

Right?

ALANA

"You being nice to your new neighbor?"

Startling at the voice, I glance up to find Marty hovering in my open office door. Beyond him and his suspenders, the lively raucous of the Friday night, after-work rush fills the air.

"Of course, I am," I say, carefully exhaling the breath I'd been holding. "I'm nice to everyone, aren't I?"

He makes a throaty sound, but the smirk on his weathered face gives him away. He knows I'm good people or he wouldn't have entrusted his store to me.

"I was just finishing the orders for next week. I was thinking we should start to bulk up on a few more things, given Labor Day is just around the corner and the rodeo is supposed to be bigger than ever this year."

Marty nods. "Yeah, I was talking with Hattie and Hazel and Char over at Wren's Café this morning. Rumor has it some there might be an ABR cameo or two this year. That could bring in a few extra spectators."

My shoulders snap back instantly at the mention of those three letters and I have to fight to keep the scowl off of my face. Mason Creek has hosted a rodeo Labor Day weekend for the past fifteen or so years and, while I don't hate it, it no longer ignites the excitement it used to. And hearing that someone big may be coming this year? Well, it doesn't take a genius to figure out who that might be and why he'd choose our little rodeo.

"You've got all of the extra orders from the rodeo vendors?" Marty asks.

"Yes, and I double-checked with everyone, too." Being such a small town, most of the local vendors order their food through the market in order to get the best bulk prices. We don't make any money on those purchases, but it's not about money when you're trying to help out friends.

Speaking of which…

"Marty, can I ask you something?"

He cocks his head to the side and leans into the door-frame. "Shoot."

"You're looking to sell sooner than later, aren't you?"

He narrows his pale blue eyes and locks them on mine. "You know that's been the plan for a while now, kiddo."

"Yeah, I know, but…" I pause, tucking a lock of hair that's escaped my ponytail behind my ear. "You've talked about it for so long now and it's always seemed like something that would happen down the road…" But he's not getting any younger and pretty soon, time is going to run out.

"I met with Grady the other day," he admits and my heart sinks. Getting a real estate agent involved is serious. Not only because it means he's more ready to sell than he's ever been, but also because listing with an agent means bigger outreach and exposure. More attention and eyes on my little store than I'm particularly comfortable with. More competition.

"Oh." It's all I can say, because the lump suddenly burning in my throat came out of nowhere.

"I know you're interested, Al. And I'd love nothing more than for this place to be yours someday. But I suspect your someday and mine aren't the same." His watery eyes are honest, but compassionate, too.

I nod, a familiar ache settling into my chest. A classic case of wanting something I'm not sure I'll be able to have. "I get it, Marty. I just... I'm going to try. I know my chances are slim, but I have a meeting with Hallie next week to discuss my options and for her to take a look at my business plan."

A small smile curls at his mouth. "Good thinking, kiddo. Real good."

Someone calls his name from the main part of the store and he glances away, smiling and lifting his hand in greeting. "It's Char," he says to me. "Gotta go solidify our plans for dinner."

"You and Char, huh?" I tease, thankful for the change in subject. "You sure she's not too feisty for you, old man?"

He makes a sound somewhere between a snort and a laugh. "Oh, she's too much, that's for damn sure. But I'm not gonna let a little detail like that stop me."

Oh, Lord. The mental image that zips through my head is not one I want to see again. Marty and Sadie's grandmother, Granny Char. It's even too much for me.

Marty flashes a quick grin before he's off chasing tail, and I return to my orders with a sigh.

As anxious as I am about Marty meeting with Grady, I'm also just as disappointed that he apparently has more of a love life than I've had in years.

Thank god, it's Friday, because this girl? She needs a long overdue drink.

***Did Hallie ask you about a girls' weekend?*** I text my best friend and Wilder's baby sister Madelyn when I finally call it a day at the market.

***Yes and I cannot wait! You're coming, right?***

***Going to try. When are you coming home next?***

She responds immediately. ***I'll be home for Labor Day for... reasons.***

I frown for a moment before it clicks. ***The rodeo? Eww. I guess I'll be hanging out by myself that weekend. Again.***

She sends a bunch of laughing emojis, but she knows I'm not kidding just like I know she's not kidding about having a thing for men in chaps.

***Anyway, I want to go out tonight, but everyone is either knocked up or busy trying to get that way.***

Mads replies, ***Sorry, sugar tits. I promise we'll go out when I'm home and I'll try to stay away from the cowboys just for you.***

I roll my eyes. ***Wow. So kind.***

Another laughing emoji pops up, followed by, ***Ask Hallie to go out with you. That girl has to need a break from my brother by now.***

I thought about Hallie, but she and I are new friends and I'm not sure we've made it to the 'let's go out' level just yet. I'd love if we ended up getting close, but her inviting me to a girls' weekend with Mads and my longtime friends is one thing. Me inviting her out to get tipsy and talk about a certain ranch hand living across the hall from me is another.

Then again, Holden does work with Wilder, so...

***Okay, I'll text her. Worst-case scenario, I chat with Emma at the bar all night.***

Mads replies with an enthusiastic, ***GET IT, GIRL!***

57

It occurs to me then that I haven't given her an update on the Holden situation. I told her Marty moved some guy in, but that was it. I feel a little guilty holding out on my best friend, but at the same time I know dang well she'd pick up on my semi-interest in a heartbeat and I'm not even sure I want to go down that road just yet.

I stare at my phone for a minute before mustering the courage to text Hallie. *I could really use a drink. Any chance you'd want to join me? My treat!*

The three dots start dancing immediately. *Funny you should mention it... Wilder, Levi, and I are headed into town for that very reason. Should be there in about 30. We'll save you a seat!*

Hallelujah! I hate that I feel like such an outcast among my friends, but it's my fault I'm in this situation. After I went through my post-Cory wild streak, I buried myself in work at the store and then my classes to try and forget about it all. Now that I'm thinking about dipping my toes back into the social pool, I can't be upset that my friends aren't latching on and dragging me in. Heck, I haven't even told them I want back in the game yet.

Maybe that changes tonight.

HOLDEN

It's barely seven o'clock and Pony Up is already rocking. The band on stage is one of the best cover bands I've heard in a while and the lead singer is one hell of an entertainer, already doing his damnedest to rile up the crowd.

"That's Tucker Simms." Wilder nods to the stage. "Works at Bumps and Dents by day, but plays here a few times a week. And that's his girl, Justine, talking with Hallie."

I follow his gaze to the bar where Hallie is talking animatedly with a brunette. They're laughing and smiling and then suddenly Hallie's gaze locks on something across the room. Her smile goes even wider and she begins waving like a fool. Naturally, I look to see what's got her so excited and I damn near fall off my stool.

"Holy shit," I mutter, and Wilder simply hums his agreement.

Alana makes her way from the entrance to the bar, carefully weaving between patrons, who occasionally give her a friendly pat on the back and more than a few bright smiles.

She's smiling just as brightly, which in and of itself isn't something I'm used to seeing. But what's really grabbed my attention is how different she looks.

I've only ever seen her in a ponytail, jeans, a tank top, and her beloved Converse, but tonight she's swapped the plain tank for an off-the-shoulder black top that's so sheer I can see the short, lacy bra number beneath it. Her hair is down too, flowing to the middle of her back in soft, dark waves, and she's swapped the sneakers for a pair of ankle boots that only seem to magnify her lush ass in another pair of snug as fuck jeans.

"Damn." Levi whistles under his breath. "Almost forgot how good she cleans up."

"Don't even think about it," Wilder grumbles. "Mads would beat your ass."

Levi laughs. "I'm not worried about our baby sister."

I smirk behind the lip of my beer before taking a pull and quietly surveying Levi a little closer. Is the interest genuine or is he simply admiring?

"Think I'm gonna get another beer," he says, tipping his head toward the ladies. "Need another round?"

Wilder nods. "Hell yeah, if you're buying."

Levi is gone a second later, sucked up into the crowd, and my focus slides back to Alana, who's visible from head to toe in a narrow sliver of space in the crowd. Seeing the opportunity for what it is, I take her in for a long, satisfying yet torturous second, adjusting in my seat when all of the blood in my body reroutes to my dick.

"Be careful, man. You keep eye-fucking her like that and she'll end up pregnant," Wilder's snarky voice quips and I tear my eyes away with a husky laugh.

"Just appreciating the view," I admit. "Something going on with her and your brother or…?"

He shakes his head. "Nah. She's our sister's best friend. Granted, he likes to mess with her, but that's all it is."

I nod and take another drink. "Good to know."

"Yeah? Why's that?" I don't have to look at Wilder to know there's a crease in his brow, but I do anyway, seeing exactly the kind of expression I'd expect from a guy who just told me the girl I'm drooling over is like a sister.

"Relax, man. I'm not looking for that kind of trouble." I offer what I hope is a light, appeasing smile, but he merely narrows his eyes. I'm pretty sure this is what he was trying to tell me last night after dinner, too.

"I'm not saying you'd be the worst guy for her, but I'm not saying you'd be the best either." He cocks an eyebrow. "You know what I mean?"

That he doesn't know me well enough to trust me just yet? Yeah, I got that. Loud and clear. And that's okay, because I already know I don't have the kind of time a girl like Alana deserves anyway. But that doesn't mean I can't flirt a little. Maybe boost her confidence a bit, because something tells me she needs it.

The telltale twang of an older country song sounds from the stage and the entire bar goes wild.

"Ohh, yeah, Mason Creek! You know what time it is! Get your sweet ass up here, woman!" The lead singer points to the woman Hallie and Alana have been talking to and she covers her face with her hands, simultaneously laughing and turning red.

"Jus-tine! Jus-tine! Jus-tine!" The crowd begins chanting her name and she makes her way to the stage, taking the lead guy's hand as he dips his head and plants a big, smacking kiss on her lips.

"Damn," I mutter, and Wilder laughs. A second later, Hallie appears in front of us, going straight to her man and toeing up for a kiss that mimics the one on the stage. "Is this a thing with this song or…?"

"Yes." Alana follows behind Hallie, pursing her lips as she rolls her eyes. "And it's disgusting."

When Tucker and his lady start belting out "Meet Me in Montana", it clicks.

"Aww, come on. It's kinda sweet, don't you think?"

Her eyes lock on mine and the faintest hint of a smile tickles at her lips before she breaks, quickly glancing toward the stage, her smile undeniable. "Whatever you say, Colorado."

"Oh, I have a nickname now? Careful, darlin', or I'm going to start thinking you like me."

She rolls her eyes but doesn't take her gaze off of the lovey-dovey couple on stage.

"If I didn't know better, I'd think you were jealous. All these couples locking lips and whatnot."

"What do you mean 'if you didn't know better'? Pretty sure you don't know me at all," she quips, bringing her mixed drink to her lips and sipping from the straw.

"I know you well enough to know you think men suck worse than those bats you're so afraid of."

Her eyebrows shoot up and she cocks her pretty head to

the side, her long hair falling over her bare shoulder. "Well, color me surprised. You've been paying attention."

"Damn right, I have." I slide off the stool and tip my head toward the bar. "I need another drink, and from the looks of it, so do you."

She glances down at the glass in her hand and twists those glossy pink lips. "Huh. I guess I do."

"I got you, darlin'." I chuckle, my hand naturally going to her waist as I shift past her. "What's your poison tonight?"

Even beneath the dim bar lights, her cheeks stain pink. "Just Malibu and pineapple."

I'm probably pushing my luck, but I lean down to her ear, enjoying the reaction far more than I should. "Anyone ever tell you how pretty you are when you blush?"

Before she can respond or even slug me for being so bold, I head for the bar.

I meant it when I told Wilder I wasn't looking for trouble here in Mason Creek, but he said it himself…

Getting to know Alana might not be the worst thing I could do.

## CHAPTER 7

ALANA

"Girl, I am so happy to see you out tonight!" Emma hollers above the music, which is still going strong well past ten o'clock.

"Well, I'm glad to be out!" I holler back to her from across the bar. She's been running her butt off all night and I wish we would have had more time to talk and catch up, but I'm glad just the same that business is booming for her. "We need to grab coffee one of these days, Em. I miss you."

Her eyes narrow suspiciously. "Are you drunk, Alana Faulkner?"

"Why would you think that?" I ask. Yes, I've had a handful of drinks and no dinner, but I'm hardly drunk.

"One, you never want to take time away from work or homework, and two, your face is flushed. Then again, maybe the color is because of that cute cowboy you've been keeping company with all night."

A wave of heat seeps into my cheeks as I glance back to

where Holden is laughing with Wilder, Levi, Caleb, Hallie, and a few other locals.

"He is cute, isn't he?" I sigh. "I mean, if I was into that kind of guy, anyway."

Emma snorts. "He couldn't be more your type if you'd designed him yourself."

"My old type," I correct her. "I don't do cowboys anymore, remember?"

"I'm not saying you have to *do* him." She laughs, handing me another drink and a bottle of Coors I don't remember ordering. "I mean, I wouldn't judge you if you did, but at the very least, you should give him this beer and ask him to dance before Tucker shuts down for the night."

Dance? I don't think so. He's growing on me, but I'm not about to draw attention to that fact and inflate his ego any more than it already is.

"Emma, can I get another round?" someone calls from down the bar and she mouths, "Ask him!" before hurrying away.

I push through the crowd, nearly dropping the drinks and falling on my ass when someone stumbles backward and crashes into me.

"Sorry about that!" the guy exclaims, but before I can tell him I'm good, an arm slides around my waist, restoring my balance.

"You all right?" Holden asks, our bodies suddenly touching in at least a dozen places.

"Yeah. Of course." I blow out a breath, force a smile, and hold up the beer. "I got you a drink."

His eyes sparkle down at me as his hold loosens, but he doesn't let go. "Thank you."

"You're welcome." I could tell him it's actually from Emma, but I like the way he's looking at me too much. I like the way he feels against me even more.

"Dance with me," he says suddenly and I shiver.

"Um, I don't know…"

The gleam in his gaze goes hazy as he leans down and says huskily, "Don't play coy. I felt that shiver."

Oh, god. Um…

"One dance," he insists, taking the drinks from my hands and setting them on our table behind us. "And then I'll leave you alone."

"Is that a promise?"

A grin slashes across his face as he laces our fingers and leads me toward the dance floor. "You'd be disappointed if it were," he says, as Tucker begins crooning a classic country ballad.

"God, you're cocky." I sigh, not bothering to fuss when one of his arms goes around my waist and the one with our tangled hands lifts beside us.

"Why haven't you danced yet tonight?" he asks quietly, his breath warm against my forehead. "I know you've wanted to."

"Oh, really?" I flick a glance up at him and he smirks.

"We've already established that I pay attention."

And I hate that he's so good at it. "Then you should know you're the first and only person to ask me to dance, so…"

"Not for lack of interest, I'll tell you that much."

I frown. "Excuse me?"

He gives a soft laugh and shakes his head. "You've had the attention of a lot of guys here tonight."

I half snort, half scoff. "Oh, please."

"I'm serious," he asserts, jutting his chin and sweeping his gaze across the crowd. "At least three of these guys tried to approach you, but for some reason, they'd get within a foot or two and chicken out."

"You're so full of shit." And frankly, this is embarrassing.

"I'm not kidding, Alana." His brows lift as he stares down at me. "Do you honestly not know?"

"Know what?"

"How fucking gorgeous you are." The words roll so easily and confidently off of his tongue that it takes a second for them to fully register. And then I blush. "You don't, do you?"

"Holden, if you're trying to get into my pants, you should know—"

"That you're the Ice Princess, right?" He gives a husky laugh as if he's figured it all out. "I thought you were being dramatic, but that's it, isn't it? You've shut them all down so many times that they're afraid to try again."

"Who's being dramatic now?" I roll my eyes and try to look anywhere but at him. Also, if Tucker could just sing the song a little faster, that'd be great, too.

Holden chuckles again and I feel the low reverberation radiate from his chest to mine. "Damn, girl. I guess I'm the luckiest guy in here tonight then, huh?"

Before I can tell him I can also make him the unluckiest, he twists my hand and pushes me away from him, twirling me out into the crowd and then promptly pulling me back. Our bodies collide and all the air from my lungs swooshes out across his face, because he's. Right. There.

"I'm onto you, darlin'," he rasps, his breath mingling with mine as his gaze lowers to my parted lips. "They're all watching us now. If you walk away and leave me standing here like a fool, you'll only confirm your reputation and I don't think that's what you want, is it?"

He has no idea what he's talking about. They don't ask me out because I'm Cory's ex and Aiden's little sister. No one wants to piss off the town celebrity or the chief deputy sheriff.

Holden smiles almost sympathetically before he lowers his head and brings his mouth so close to my ear that his lips brush my skin. "Maybe I can help you," he whispers and something about the featherlike caress of his mouth and just him in general has goose bumps rising everywhere.

"H-help me?" I stammer, my eyes fluttering shut as my hand balls in the fabric of his T-shirt at the small of his back.

"Uh huh." He nuzzles close and the second the stubble on his jaw abrades my neck, I'm a goner. "Let's make 'em think you're into me. Show them the ice is melting."

Ice? What ice? All I feel is heat. So. Damn. Much. Heat.

By the time the song is over, I don't even know where I am anymore. My senses have gone all haywire and all I can say is it's a damn good thing Holden is still holding my hand or I might very well collapse in a pool of lust right in the middle of Pony Up.

"We're gonna get out of here," he tells Wilder and Hallie as we approach the table, where our drinks still sit untouched.

"Oh." Hallie glances from me to him and back again, a slight crease in her brow. "You didn't drive, did you?"

"No." I shake my head, which has started to become a little cloudy. Probably equal parts buzz and whatever the hell just happened with Holden. "I walked."

"Me, too," Holden speaks up, tucking me into his side. "I'll get her home safely."

Wilder clears his throat and sniffs and when I glance up at him, I get the distinct feeling he isn't thrilled. "You feeling all right, Al?"

I nod. "Yeah. I'm, uh, actually I'm kind of hungry, so we're going to grab a pizza from Sauce It Up before they close."

I flick a glance up to Holden, hoping he'll play along, and he does, nodding like we'd already discussed it.

I glance back to Hallie and Wilder as relief washes over both of their faces.

"Ah, okay." Wilder nods. "Yeah, you'd better get moving then. They close soon."

"Thanks for tonight," I tell Hallie when she pulls me in for a quick hug.

"I'm glad you came out." She holds on for an extra second, whispering, "He seems like a nice guy, but be careful, okay?"

I give a quick nod and she lets go. Two minutes later, Holden and I step outside into the warm night, and I suck in a deep breath, still trying to process what the heck is going on. But then my stomach growls and getting something to eat is suddenly more important than figuring it out.

"I really am hungry," I admit, my hand pressed to my belly. "In fact, I'm going to hate myself tomorrow if I don't eat."

He chuckles and reaches for my hand again. "I said I'd get you home safely and that includes making sure you're fed. Where exactly are we going?"

"Sauce It Up is in the town square, so…" I spin to the left and point to the street. "We go that way."

"All right then." He winks down at me and we spend the next few minutes making our way toward the town square. "Pretty quiet this time of night, huh?"

"Yeah, most of the town shuts down around dinnertime, save the places to grab a bite to eat or a beer." I point out Dream Big, which is our local real estate agency, the barbershop, the florist, and Java Jitters. "Java has the absolute best coffee around. If coffee is your thing, that is. Is it? Coffee, I mean?"

Holden laughs. "I like coffee, but have gone without for the last few days, since I haven't picked up a coffee pot yet."

"Oh, no." As a certified coffee-aholic, I feel his loss deep in my bones. "What time do you get up in the morning?"

"I've been getting to the ranch around five or five thirty. Is the coffee shop open then?"

Crap. "Unfortunately, no. But…" I give his hand a little tug. "You just happen to have a neighbor who is usually up at that time and always has coffee on. I bet she could hook you up."

He grins down at me as we turn the corner and the Italian restaurant and pizzeria, still lit up like Christmas, comes into view. "Oh, you tell me this now?" he asks, nudging me playfully with his elbow.

"I didn't like you before," I admit, leaning back into him just as casually.

"But you do now?" His steps slow a bit as we approach the entrance.

"I mean, you're okay. Though I'm not entirely sure what you think is going on with me and the guys in town. You're going to have to explain that to me."

He dips his chin. "Let's grab our pizza and then I'll do just that."

HOLDEN

"You weren't lying. This pizza is pretty damn good." Leaning forward on Alana's couch, I snag another piece from the box on her coffee table.

"Told you," she says around a bite, holding the back of her hand to her mouth as she sits cross-legged on the floor on the other side of the table. "It's almost as good as sex. Maybe better."

I choke on the gigantic bite I just took, quickly reaching for the bottle of beer she'd offered me to go along with our late night dinner. "What?" I finally ask, eyes still watering.

"You heard me." She glances up at me with a mischievous

glint in her eye. A glint I'm sure is more than partly fueled by all of the Malibu she drank tonight.

"Uh, I'm not sure I agree." Because as far as I'm concerned, there isn't anything in the world better than sex. And if she's seriously comparing the down and dirty to pizza, she obviously hasn't been doing it with anyone worth a shit.

"Then again, maybe it's just been so long I don't remember." She sighs and takes another bite, closing her eyes and giving a little moan as she does.

I watch her for a moment, the pieces of the puzzle that is Alana Faulkner slowly snapping into place. The grudge against men, the icy shield she keeps locked in place, the guys in town being so gun-shy around her... "How long are we talking?"

She flicks a glance my way as she swallows. "I'm pretty much a reborn virgin."

Well, shit. I adjust from side to side on the couch, my jeans suddenly snug. "Really."

She laughs softly. "TMI?"

I grin, take another bite, and ponder the confession for a moment. "I wouldn't say TMI."

"Surprising?"

I shake my head. "Not really. I mean, it's all starting to make sense, if I'm honest."

"What do you mean?" She cocks her head to the side, her hair falling off her shoulder in waves, as I finish off the last of my slice and take a pull from my beer.

"Well, you more or less introduced yourself as the Ice Princess. Then the way the guys acted like they were about to piss themselves just thinking about talking to you tonight. It wasn't hard to figure out."

She narrows her eyes above a smirk. "What exactly do you think you've figured out?"

"My guess is that Megatron of exes, as you called him,

hurt you pretty badly and you threw yourself into working at the store and school, essentially deeming yourself off-limits."

Her smile evaporates like water on hot asphalt. "Dang."

I watch her as she sets her plate on the table and seems to zone out uncomfortably for a moment. "Someone local?"

She's quiet as she picks at the hem of her blouse. "He was, but he doesn't live here anymore."

Good, because I already hate the asshole. "What did he do?"

"Cheated. I'm aware of three girls, but there were probably more."

Son of a bitch.

"Can we talk about something else? Something less depressing?" She glances up, her whiskey eyes hopeful, instead of sad or hurt.

"Sure. What'd you have in mind?"

She lifts a shoulder. "I don't know. Tell me about your family maybe."

"Okay." I lean back on the couch and stretch my arm across the back. "I have two younger siblings, a brother and sister. Kaden is twenty-three and Tessa is twenty-one. My mom and dad will celebrate their thirtieth anniversary this year. My dad's worked as a foreman at my uncle's ranch just as long, and Mom retired last year. She was a nurse at an assisted living facility."

Alana's eyebrows lift. "Is your uncle's ranch the one you worked at?"

"Not recently, no. I did grow up working there, though."

She smiles softly. "Ah, so it really is in your blood, then."

I chuckle and tap my beer bottle against my knee. "You could say that."

"Did you go to college or anything? Or was it always ranch life?"

"I went to college for a couple of years. Got an associate's degree in agricultural science. You know, just in case."

"Just in case?"

"In case I ever wanted to have my own animals someday."

"Is that something you want? You know, someday?"

Damn, she cut straight to the heart of things, didn't she? "Maybe? I'm not sure. I've been pretty content with how things have been. Haven't thought much about it." But if the ABR doesn't get their head out of their ass, I'll probably have to think about it sooner than later. "How about you? Do you have anyone other than Aiden?"

She gets up from the floor and takes a seat on the other end of the worn, but comfortable couch, her knees folded in front of her. She's still dressed in her jeans and see-through top, but she's lost the boots and her feet are bare, pretty pink toenails peeking up at me.

"My mom and dad own a farm on the outskirts of town. Nothing huge, but big enough to pay the bills. Unfortunately, I don't see them as often as I'd like because of work and school, but it's nice knowing they're close. And I'm sure you know that Aiden's just recently come back to Mason Creek from L.A."

I did not know that. We'd only met a few times out on the road over the years, and I guess I hadn't paid much attention to where he was living at the time. I just knew that he and Cory were old high school pals.

"My best friend Madelyn is Wilder and Levi's sister. She's off finishing her master's degree right now. I'm close with Aiden's fiancée, Emma, too. Mads and Emma are basically like the sisters I never had."

"I think you'd like my sister Tessa. She's a smart-ass just like you."

"Hey!" She reaches out and pokes at my arm, still stretched across the couch. "Growing up around all of these

Mason Creek guys forced me to become the way I am. It's a survival mechanism."

"And now they're scared shitless of you."

"What the heck are you talking about?" She laughs, but there's a guarded glint in her eye, too.

"I saw it at least five times tonight. You had your back turned to them, so you didn't see, but I watched them make their way over to you only to stop short of actually tapping on your shoulder and asking you to dance."

She rolls her eyes. "You are so full of shit."

"Why would I lie to you about that?" I laugh.

"Oh, I don't know. Maybe to catch me off guard and give you an excuse to make a move yourself?"

I smirk behind the lip of my beer. "Is it working?"

She swats at my arm. "Holden McMurray, don't you dare mess with me. I'll keep that bathroom locked permanently."

I only laugh harder. "Oh, is that how we're going to play this?"

"Just be real with me!" she says, throwing her hands in the air and letting them drop to her lap. "I've been screwed over one too many times. I don't know what's real and what isn't anymore."

My chuckle softens as our eyes meet again. "I am being real, Alana."

Her eyes dart back and forth between mine. "Why would they not ask me?" she finally asks, her tone almost disappointed.

"Like I said before, you've probably shot them down before."

She gulps, and in the near silence of her apartment, I hear it.

"Did you ever date anyone else from Mason Creek or just the asshole ex?"

She eyes me for a quiet moment. "Why are you so interested in my love life?"

"Something tells me you need a friend. Maybe I can be that for you. At least while I'm here."

"Why would you want to do that?"

"Because I like you."

Her eyes widen. Initially, it's in surprise, but I see hope there, too.

"I could be wrong, but from what you've told me yourself and what I've gathered from bits of conversation with your brother and Wilder, you've thrown yourself into work and school and you've more or less cut yourself off from any kind of social life."

She swallows again. "It's not necessarily a bad thing."

"For a short while, no. I'm sure it's served its purpose. But it can't go on forever, and something tells me you're ready for it to end."

She studies me for a long moment, her eyes sliding around my face as if she's searching for something, but can't quite figure out what. "And you think you can help me with that?"

I dip my chin. "Yes, ma'am."

"How?"

A crooked grin tugs at my mouth. "Well, darlin', I think we got a pretty good start tonight. For one, you came out. Then you danced with me." I give her a sly smile and gesture around her apartment. "And then you took me home."

She gasps. "But I didn't… This isn't…" She flounders for the right words and I chuckle, reaching for her hand.

"I know that, darlin'. But that doesn't mean we can't let them think otherwise." I bring her hand to my mouth and kiss her knuckles slow and sweet. She sighs. "All we gotta do is let them see us together a few times. Let them think you're into me and me you."

"But if they think I like you, how does that help me?"

"I'm only here for a few weeks, darlin'. Someone's gotta sweep in and heal your broken heart when I'm gone." I wink and a small smile flits across her face.

"My broken heart, huh?"

"Don't worry, gorgeous, I'll be gentle."

# CHAPTER 8

ALANA

"*R*umor has it you and a certain mysterious cowboy were seen canoodling in the town square last night."

I snap upright behind the service counter, a roll of receipt paper in hand, to find Tate Michaels smirking at me with a brown paper bag full of groceries on her hip. As one of Mason Creek's biggest gossips and author of The MC Scoop, her comment sends an instant wave of dread through me.

"Canoodling?" I roll my eyes and go to work replacing the paper in the register. "We were walking home from Pony Up."

"Home?" Her brows lift and I curse under my breath. "So, it's true he's living above the store with you?"

"Not *with* me," I correct her and consider whether or not I should explain about the small room, but honestly, what was the point? She was going to spin the story how she wanted to regardless.

"He's cute." She flashes a genuine smile and for a fleeting

second, I wonder if she's simply making friendly conversation instead of digging for dirt. Then I remember that there's no line for Tate. No boundaries. Anything and everything goes, because just like I need money for my bills, so does she.

"Hmm." My only response is a hum as I try to pretend I'm not already dreading her next headline.

"Anyway, it's good to see you dating again," she offers with a shrug before she heads off toward the exit, quickly falling into step with none other than Hazel Jackson.

Great. Just freaking great.

Then again, maybe that's exactly what I need. At least, if I'm going to actually do this thing with Holden. Which I'm not sure that I am.

As if on cue, my phone lights up on the counter with a text from the devil himself. Quickly snapping the receipt roll back into place, I snatch up my cell and thumb to the message.

*Wilder said he's not paying me any more overtime this week, so I'll be home early. Wanna grab dinner and give this town something to talk about?*

Oh, they're already talking. Or at least they will be as soon as Tate whips up her article.

*You really want to do this?* I text back.

*Hell yes. I mean, spend a little time with a pretty lady or spend my Saturday night on a crappy bed, playing on my phone? Not a tough choice, darlin'.*

I laugh to myself, my cheeks heating at the compliment and the realization that he's serious about helping me. And maybe because he's not exactly hard to look at, either.

*Okay, I'm down. Where are you thinking?*
*Wren's Café. Five o'clock okay?*
*Perfect. See you after work?*
*Looking forward to it.*

Excitement warring with nerves in my stomach, I close out of my phone and set it aside.

Truthfully, I have no idea what I'm doing with Holden. He isn't wrong that I've been feeling all sorts of restless lately. That seeing my friends so happy and in love isn't slowly eating away at me and making me question so many of the decisions I've made. But is playing this game with him really the right approach? I'd be happy to simply have my friends again. I don't necessarily need romance, though I wouldn't be averse to it, either.

God, that's a crazy thought. Me in the dating game again. It's been such a long time that the concept seems so foreign, yet I can't keep the smile from my face. Especially when I think about getting my feet wet again with someone like Holden.

I know, I know. He isn't sticking around and he's only offered to help kick-start my social life again. But…

Would it really hurt to enjoy myself a little during the process?

---

"Dang, Colorado, you clean up nice." I can't help but smile at the handsome cowboy standing outside my door. Jeans, a snug black T-shirt, and a perfectly broken-in Stetson to match. "You smell good too," I add, though I already knew he would. The fresh, citrusy aroma of his body wash had been wafting into my apartment for the past twenty minutes, while he showered.

Holden tucks his hands into his pockets and chuckles, his eyes dancing over my flowing top and skinny jeans, before he dips his chin. "Looking pretty good yourself, darlin'. I really like when you leave your hair down."

I touch a hand to the mess of waves draped over my

shoulder as familiar warmth spreads over my skin. "Thank you."

"You ready to go?" He tips his head toward the stairs and I nod, grabbing my purse and closing the door behind me. As soon as we're outside, he reaches for my hand.

"You okay with walking again? I figured everyone would be on a nice day like this. Might catch a few more eyes." He winks and I press my lips together in a smirk.

"You're taking this awfully seriously, Colorado."

"Something you should know about me... I don't half-ass anything, darlin'."

"I see." I let him lace our fingers and lead me around the rear corner of the market and onto Old Bridge Road. Cars pass by in the street ahead of us in the town square, and I suck in a nervous breath. "You should probably know that people are already talking about us. In fact, there's this online thing—"

"The MC Scoop?"

My steps falter a bit as I blink up at him. "You've heard of it?"

"Found it when I was playing around on my phone and looking for the local news the other day. Ain't nothing sacred around here, is there?"

I laugh. "Not a thing."

"Gotta love small towns." He chuckles as we fall into stride, the warm evening breeze flitting around us. "So you said you grew up here?"

"Yep. I'm a Mason Creek lifer. Wasn't what I'd planned, but here I am."

He gives my hand a reassuring squeeze. "Nothing wrong with coming home, darlin'. Especially not to a place like this."

"No, though, if I'm honest, I wasn't thrilled about the decision when I first made it."

"Why did you then?"

Because I was a foolish, broken-hearted girl who thought she had no other choice? "Just seemed like what I needed," I say instead.

"You came back after you broke up with Megatron, right?"

Wait, did I tell him that or did he hear it from Wilder. Either way… "It's embarrassing, but yeah. I was lucky to have made it through the end of the semester."

"Nothing to be embarrassed about. Shit happens sometimes. The important thing is that we don't let it get so far under our skin that it changes us."

I give a nervous laugh. "Yeah, about that…"

He flicks a glance my way. "What about it?"

I hesitate for a moment, not sure I want to confess my biggest weakness to a guy a barely know. But then I remember he's only here for a short time, so what does it matter?

"I definitely let it change me," I confess, reaching up to tuck a lock of hair behind my ear as the breeze blows and a car horn honks in the distance. "I am one-hundred-percent certain I wouldn't be here in Mason Creek right now if it hadn't been for C—" I stop short, not wanting to say his name out loud. "If it hadn't been for the breakup."

In my peripheral, Holden's eyes narrow slightly before he nods. "Ah."

"See? Embarrassing." I laugh again, but there's nothing funny about it. I hate that I gave so much of myself to Cory. I hate even more that I had no idea I'd built so much of my life around his aspirations until he was gone and I was left struggling to figure out mine.

"Nah, darlin', I think you've gotta flip how you're thinking about this." He gives my hand a squeeze as we near the town square. "It might seem like you changed course because of him, but I think in your heart of hearts, you came here because you knew you belonged here."

"Hmm." I give a skeptical smile and he chuckles.

"Let me ask you this…" We slow to a stop at the intersection in front of the bank and he turns to face me. "Is there someplace else you'd rather be instead right now?"

"Not really."

"You don't regret not living in the big city? Working some fancy corporate job?"

I laugh. "Definitely not. I like being close to my parents, even though I don't see them as often as I should. And now Aiden is here, too. My friends…" I sigh and he cocks his head to the side.

"So this isn't about the place you're living in—it's about how you're living."

Damn, he's good. "How are you this perceptive?"

"I've always had a knack for figuring people out, darlin'." He winks and leans down to brush a kiss across my cheek just as a police cruiser pulls up to the intersection, the passenger window already rolled down.

"What the hell is this?" Aiden barks from the driver's seat. I bristle and try to drop Holden's hand, but he holds on tight.

"Just taking your sister to dinner," he says as he turns to face my brother, who's now leaning across the console to get a better look at us.

"Why?" Aiden snaps, brow creased.

"Because we're hungry?" Holden chuckles like being busted by my brother is no big deal. Or maybe because he knows it is and doesn't care.

"You hold hands with everyone you have dinner with?" My brother lifts his chin to our joined hands and my face is so hot, it might burst into flames. It isn't that he's caught me with a guy, but rather because he thinks this is real and part of me is embarrassed that it's not.

"No offense, Faulkner, but how I treat my dates is none of your concern. Unless it's illegal to be sweet on a girl in public in Mason Creek, which I'm pretty sure it's not, given the way you were tongue wrestling yours the other day at the bar."

Aiden's expression falls and his jaw sets tight. I expect him to have another smart-ass comeback, but he doesn't say anything. He just glares at me for a long moment, before he bites off a curse and drives away.

"Is he always this uptight about you dating?" Holden asks as we watch Aiden's taillights.

"I have no idea. I haven't dated in forever, remember?"

Holden sticks his tongue in his cheek and nods, almost to himself. "He'll be out at the ranch tomorrow to read me the riot act, no doubt about it."

Crap. "I'm sorry. We don't have to do this…"

Holden turns to me again, his brows raised above a lopsided grin. "Don't think you'll get rid of me that easily, darlin'. I made a commitment to you and I fully intend to follow through."

"Yes, but I don't want my brother hating you for something that isn't even real."

Mischief flashes in his eyes and he takes a step closer. So close, in fact, that his chest touches mine and my traitorous nipples pebble at his heat. "We might be playing around, but rest assured, beautiful… when I touch you, I do it because I want to, not because it's part of the game."

"O-oh," I squeak, and Holden chuckles as he leans down and presses a kiss to my forehead.

"Let's get to the café and get you fed. If your brother is going to hate me, it sure as hell isn't going to be for starving you."

# CHAPTER 9

HOLDEN

*W*e arrive at Wren's a few minutes later and the waitress seats us at one of the bistro-style tables near the front of the diner. She comes back with our drinks and we give her our food order, but she no sooner walks away than Alana gasps and quickly turns toward the window, shielding her face.

"What? Are you hiding from someone?" I chuckle.

"Mmm hmm."

"Who?" My gaze shifts to the door where an older couple has just entered, followed by a dark-haired guy in a dark green polo, dark jeans, and a pair of aviator sunglasses. Given the couple is in their eighties and completely harmless, my money is on the guy. "Him?"

"Shh!" she hisses, shooting me a quick 'I will kill you if you draw attention' glare. Of course, I grin, because she's obviously forgotten that drawing attention to her is my new job.

"Is he the ex?" I ask, lowering my voice and trying to

check out the guy in my peripheral. He's yet to look our way as he talks with a waitress at the cash register.

"No!" she spits, then mutters, "Not the one you're thinking of anyway."

My eyebrows lift. "Oh, really?"

She glances up just long enough for me to spot the color in her cheeks.

"You got a little history you forgot to mention, darlin'?"

She rolls her eyes and opens her mouth to say something when a masculine voice sounds from a few feet away.

"Alana? Is that you?"

I don't need to look to know we've been seen, and Alana's whimper confirms it.

"Haven't seen you outside of the market in forever," he adds.

I glance to our left as the guy strolls over with a take-out bag in hand. His sunglasses hang from the collar of his shirt and his eyes are locked on my date like I'm not even here. Something about that rubs me the wrong way, but I'm far more interested in figuring out why Alana hoped to avoid him.

"Uh, hi, Cole." She pastes on a smile, barely flicking it his way. "How are you?"

"I'm great." He takes her in without shame, his cocky grin hitching a little higher on one side, clearly liking what he sees. "You look good, babe. Love what you've done with your hair."

*Babe?* Another wave of something unsettling rolls through me and I clench my fist against my thigh as I remind myself that this isn't a real date and I have no friggin' right to want to punch this guy for flirting with my girl.

"Thank you. Um, this is Holden." Alana's pleading, but hopeful eyes meet mine across the table as she gestures my way. "Holden, this is Cole Jackson. He works at Dream Big. He's also a Mason Creek lifer."

"Ah." I think what she meant to say is they go back, and not in a platonic sort of way. Despite wanting to jab my fist into his gut, I offer my hand. "Nice to meet you, Cole."

He accepts with a smirk. "You're the new guy out at the ranch, right?"

"Yup." I can't quite read the grin, so I'm not sure if he's trying to be a condescending prick or if it's just his style. "Alana's new neighbor, too."

I swear to God I hear her gulp across the table.

"Is that so?" Cole shifts his focus back to her. "Glad to see you doing something other than work, but I'm not going to lie—I'm a little jealous that you're having dinner with this guy and not me."

Yeah, well, when you're the type of guy who interrupts other people's dates to try and score one of your own, no wonder the ladies don't want you, dude.

Alana blinks. "We're just—"

"We hit it off right away," I interject, covering her hand with mine. "And who am I to decline time with a pretty lady?"

The guy's brows lift and then he clears his throat. "That's… that's really great, Al."

She nods a little too eagerly. "Yeah, um, it is. Listen, it was really great seeing you again."

That's my girl. Get him the hell out of here.

Cole dips his chin, clearly getting the message, and then glances back to me. "Nice to meet you, Holden. Be good to her, okay? She's special."

I can't resist winking. "Believe me, I've already figured that out."

The guy eyes me for a second longer before saying goodbye to Alana and then leaving the diner. The door is

85

barely closed behind him when Alana's shoe connects with my shin under the table.

"A little overkill, don't you think?"

I laugh. "The guy was ready to swoop you up and carry you off to his lair like I wasn't even here."

"Cole is the town flirt. He's like that with everyone."

"Yeah, but the two of you have done more than flirt, haven't you? You said something about him not being the ex I was thinking of, so obviously, you've dated."

Her face turns as red as the plastic cup holding her Diet Dr. Pepper. "I wouldn't say that."

"Ohh. I see." I tip my head back and laugh. "I thought you said it'd been a while?"

"It has. But can we… can we just not?" Alana pleads, head hung low again. "It was a post-breakup thing and clearly not my best decision."

"It's nothing to be ashamed of, darlin'. We all do shit we wish we could take back. And some of us do shit we'd happily do all over again, too. It's part of life. Gives us character, too."

She eyes me reluctantly from beneath her lashes. "You don't think less of me?"

"Darlin', I may come off as old fashioned because I'm all chivalrous and shit, but don't think for a second I'd ever judge you for having a little fun."

A small smile flits across her lips before she bites at one corner. "We've talked far too much about me already tonight and we haven't even gotten our food yet."

I stroke my thumb over her knuckles. "I like talking about you."

"Yes, but it's hardly fair. Tell me something about you."

"Like what?"

She narrows her eyes for a second and then asks bluntly, "You've had lots of one-night stands, haven't you?"

I damn near choke on my own saliva. "Damn, girl, just go straight for my jugular, why don't you?"

She laughs softly. "No shame, Colorado. Besides, you just said it gives us character." She adds a wink and I pull my hand away from hers to scrub it over my face, laughing right along with her.

"Maybe we shouldn't talk about sex," I say. "At least not in public where anything and everything we say has a fifty-fifty chance of ending up in a gossip column."

She snorts. "True, though I'm sure we've given them plenty of fodder already, especially with Cole coming over."

"Eh, I'm used to people talking shit about me. This is nothing."

Her eyes go wide before I realize my screwup. "Oh?"

Shit. "You know how small towns are," I say, quickly redirecting.

"You've been the talk of the town back in Bear Creek, too? Maybe I should Google you." She reaches for her phone, but I grab her hand again.

"How about you just ask me?" I ask, cursing myself the second the words leave my mouth. I don't want her looking me up and finding out shit that might scare her away, but I certainly don't want to bullshit my way around the truth, either. I like this girl too much to lie to her any more than I already have to.

"Okay..." She pauses as the waitress arrives and sets our plates in front of us. When she's out of earshot, Alana asks, "Why have people talked shit about you, Holden McMurray?"

I unwrap my utensils and put the napkin on my lap before cutting my chicken parmesan. "Like I told you, Bear Creek is a small town, too. Let's just say... well, let's just say I'm well known."

"For being a playboy?"

I give a laugh, but it fades quickly when I realize she's being serious and not in a judgmental way.

"I wish it were just that." Having a reputation as a player is a hell of a lot less threatening than being accused of sexual assault. "Let's just say I know some people who've tried to use their social status to get what they want, no matter the consequences or impact it might have on others."

Her brow creases as she tears a chicken tender in half to cool. "And by 'others', you mean you? Or maybe your family?"

"Just me, thankfully." If I hadn't been cleared right away, my family probably would have felt the impact, too. So, as much as this whole thing sucks, I know it could have been a lot worse.

"Does this have anything to do with the ranch you were working on?" she asks.

Fuck. There are only so many ways I can answer her questions without giving too much away or blatantly lying.

"No." I stab another bite onto my fork, pop it into my mouth, and chew for a ridiculously long moment, trying to come up with something better. But I can't, because there isn't anything. I can't lie to her about this. "What would you say if I told you I'd been accused of something I didn't do?"

She lifts a shoulder, her expression unfazed. "I feel like I know you well enough to give you the benefit of the doubt. If you say you didn't do it, I believe you didn't."

Was she for real? "You've known me for a matter of days."

"You've not only offered to help break me out of the Fort Knox of sad social lives, but you saved me from becoming a vampire princess too, remember?"

I chuckle. "How could I forget?"

"So, what have you been wrongfully accused of?" she asks before I can even finish my question. "If you don't mind me asking."

"If I tell you, you have to promise me you won't Google me later. Your brother and Wilder know everything and I can guaran-damn-tee that if Aiden thought you had anything to worry about, he would've beat my ass in the street earlier. More than that, he wouldn't have suggested I move in next door to you."

Her curious eyes dance back and forth between mine. "Okay. I won't look if you don't want me to."

"Seriously?"

She nods. "Seriously."

"Wow." It's not that I don't believe her. It's that I do believe her and, after so many people have turned their back on me, her trust means more than I would have expected.

This time, she's the one to reach across the table and take my hand. "No shame and no judgment, Colorado."

Well, shit. I set down my fork and swallow. There's no good way to say it that will make it sound any less awful than it is, so I just come out with it.

"I was accused of forcing myself on a girl. The only issue with her claim was that I was in another state at the time. I was arrested at home but cleared less than six hours later. Unfortunately, the girl is from a well-off family and the media wasted no time dragging my name through the mud anyway."

She wets her lips and I can tell she's trying so damn hard not to react. "That's awful, Holden. I'm so sorry."

"Yeah, me too. It's been one hell of a month."

"Is that why you were laid off? Does your boss not believe you?"

Dammit. I need to tell her the truth about what I do for a living, too, but with the way gossip runs rampant in this town, I can't risk telling her just yet. Especially not out in public where anyone could hear and leak my real name to that damn gossip site.

I pull in a deep breath. "He believes me, but he isn't a fan of the drama. He forced me to take a voluntary leave of absence until things settle down."

"Things being?"

"The media mostly." They might've moved on from the accusations, but they're still curious about why the ABR decided to ostracize one of their biggest stars despite being cleared.

"Jesus," she murmurs. "Sounds worse than the Mason Creek gossip grapevine."

"Yup." I force a smile and fork up another bite. "I can't believe you're not freaking out right now."

"Why would I freak out?" She frowns and dips a piece of chicken into a small container of honey mustard.

"I just told you I was arrested for assault."

"And you told me you didn't do it."

I study her for a long moment, trying to figure out if she's really as cool about the confession as she's trying to appear or if she's going to add a few more locks to her door as soon as we get home.

"You're really something," I say, mimicking words she's said herself and deciding to be grateful instead of skeptical.

Alana smirks. "A good something or a bad something?"

"Definitely a good something." Something I really never expected to find here in this sleepy little town, but here we are.

# CHAPTER 10

ALANA

"**W**hat in the hell is going on with you and Holden?" Aiden demands as soon as I accept his call bright and early Sunday morning. I expected he'd call last night or blow up my phone with a bunch of texts, so the fact that he managed to hold back a solid twelve hours is impressive.

"Good morning, dearest brother. How'd you sleep last night?" I ask, ignoring his question while I make a pot of coffee.

"Don't try to change the subject," he grumbles. "You go from complete lockdown to gallivanting all over town with this guy. For fuck's sake, he's been here five days."

I laugh and tug my robe a little tighter around myself. "For one, we've only officially gone out once. The other time, he was just walking me home from Pony Up. And two, you were the one who made him my neighbor, so if you're going to get cranky with anyone, it should be yourself."

He makes a throaty sound, and in the background, I hear

his cruiser start. "Yeah, but I figured you'd been living like a nun, so I wouldn't have anything to worry about."

"Oh, Aiden." Another laugh rises.

He's quiet for a moment and I imagine he's backing out of his driveway, heading to work. "Look, he's a nice guy, but there are some things—"

"He told me."

My brother gasps. "He did?"

"Yes, and I'm pretty sure you wouldn't allow a guy with a dirty background to move in next to me, so I know you're not worried about it."

He's silent for another beat. "He told you about the assault accusation."

I close my eyes and press my fingers to my forehead, a headache already starting and it's barely five in the morning. "Yes, Aiden. He told me. God, you're a pain in the butt sometimes."

I can hear him swallow through the line. "Did he say anything else?"

Oh my god. "Like what? That he's a serial killer and plans to chop me into a million pieces? No, Aid. We've talked about a lot of things, but his plan to put me out of my misery wasn't one of them."

"Alana…" Aiden's tone is a mix of annoyance and warning.

"Look, I know you haven't had to play the protective big brother role in a while, but please don't think you need to start now."

"I'm not trying to warn you off of him, Al. I'm just saying there are probably some things you should know."

"And I hear you. But here's the thing—I don't need to know everything about him. He's only here for a few weeks and I just want to let loose and have some fun. Is that really such a bad thing?"

A low, rumbling sound slides through the line and I roll my eyes, already knowing what's to come. "Fun?" he spits. "What the hell kind of fun are we talking about?"

"Nope." I laugh, grabbing a mug as the coffee pot stops brewing. "*We* aren't talking about it whatsoever."

He pulls in an audible breath, surely preparing to lecture me on how I better not be banging my new neighbor, when the bathroom door opens and a freshly showered Holden steps into my apartment.

"'Morning," he says, his voice still rough from sleep. Just like it had been yesterday when he stopped by for coffee before heading to the ranch.

"He spent the fucking night?" Aiden roars.

I don't even bother clarifying. Instead, I wink at Holden and point to the phone. "Aiden says good morning."

Holden's eyebrows dart up and a sly smirk plays across his lips. "Good morning, Faulkner," he taunts, leaning into the phone as he pops the top off of his travel mug.

I clamp a hand over my mouth to keep from laughing as Aiden snarls, "I'm going to kill him."

"No, you aren't. You like your job too much for that. Anyway, I have to get going. I have extra donuts to frost this morning for the church crowd. Thanks for calling to check in."

"Alana," Aiden warns again, but my finger is already hovering over the end button.

"Love you, Aid! Have a great day!" Before he can argue, I click off the call with a lighthearted sigh. "Well, that was fun."

"He called you already this morning?" Holden chuckles.

"Yep. Must've stewed about it all night and couldn't wait any longer."

"What'd he say?"

"That you're dead."

Holden grunts a laugh. "Yep, he'll definitely be paying me a visit today."

"I'm sorry."

"Why?" He turns to face me and leans a denim-clad hip against the counter, the delicious scent of his body wash wafting over me in the best kind of way. His dark gray T-shirt fits him just like the black one did last night—snug in all the right places. "I signed up for this, darlin', remember?"

"Actually, I don't recall you signing up to be harassed by my brother for a relationship we're not even in."

A small smile tickles at his lips as his gaze slips down to the V of my robe, then my bare legs, and back up again. "I'd say the perks more than make up for it."

"The perks?"

He reaches out and trails a rough fingertip from my collarbone down to the once again gaping V in my robe. "Getting to see you like this first thing in the morning is one hell of a way to start the day, darlin'."

*Gulp.*

"We still on for a picnic this afternoon?"

"Uh, yeah." If I don't self-combust before then. "Providing Aiden doesn't kill you first."

He winks as he heads for the door. "Let him try, babe."

HOLDEN

"Why the hell is Aiden Faulkner texting me at five thirty on a Sunday morning?" Wilder holds up his phone as soon as I hop out of my truck at the ranch.

"I don't know." I chuckle. "Maybe because he thinks I spent the night with his sister?"

"*Did* you spend the night with her?" my friend asks, eyes wide and chin lowered, like he's ready to rain hellfire on me, too.

"Of course, not. What the hell kind of guy do you think I am?"

"The kind with a dick?"

Laughing, I grab my lunch box and water from my back seat and toss it into the ranch truck. "You got me there."

"What are you doing with Alana, man? Just cut the shit and just be straight with me. I saw how you two were at Pony Up last Friday night. I know you're into her."

"And if I am?"

"You gotta tell her who you are. Before shit gets out of hand."

"Aren't you the one who told me not to tell anyone?"

His expression falls and he pulls in a breath. "That was before you even came to town and when I didn't think it mattered. But if you're going to do more than share her bathroom…" He leaves the rest unsaid while I grab my gloves and Stetson.

"Yeah, I know." I slap the gloves against my palm. "I almost told her last night, but we were at the diner and I didn't want anyone overhearing. The last thing I need is for that damn gossip column to post my name and location and for the media to spin this like I'm hiding out like a guilty bastard."

Wilder nods. "I get it. But don't fuck around with this. And trust me when I say she'll cut you out of her life faster than a Burdizzo on a set of nuts if she finds out the truth from someone else."

"I'll tell her." Not because he's telling me to, but because it's the right thing to do.

"Good. Because I'd hate to have to kick your ass if you don't."

WILDER AND I spent all day in Rebel River helping out an old friend of his, who recently acquired full responsibility of the ranch her deceased husband had run for decades. She's a firecracker of a lady and she knows her way around, but she doesn't have the best relationship with the ranch manager and that's made things tense.

"Wouldn't be surprised if Sandy put the place up for sale soon," Wilder muses as we pull back into the Roman Wilde Ranch later that afternoon. "Her heart isn't in it now that Hank is gone and she's not the type to roll over and let Dean run the show. Not with the way he disrespects her like he does."

Yeah, I wasn't impressed with the guy, either. Something about him rubbed me the wrong way and then he opened his mouth and cocked off to the woman who now signs his paychecks. Wasn't cool in the least.

"It's a hell of a spread. Damn near as nice as Roman Wilde."

Wilder grins. "Nothing's as nice as the RWR."

I laugh. "I mean, it's all right…"

He throws a fist across the console and smacks me in the chest before flipping me off and hopping out… just as Aiden Faulkner pulls up in his cruiser.

"Fuck," I grumble and Wilder just laughs.

"You asked for it, McMurray, now take your punishment."

I want to tell him that I didn't technically do anything wrong, because Alana and I aren't really dating, but then I remember the way I'd held her hand and kissed her a cheek a couple of times and laid in bed with my hand around my dick, thinking about her.

"McMurray," the broody cop grumbles as he

approaches. He's dressed casually enough in a pair of jeans and MCSO polo, but the gun strapped to his hip is all business.

"Faulkner," I greet him in return, grabbing my stuff from the ranch truck.

"You got something you want to tell me?" he asks, coming to stand a little too close with his hands on his hips and fire in his eyes.

"Not particularly, no." I flash a cocky smirk and take my chances turning my back on him to stow my stuff away in my own truck.

"Are you messing around with my sister?" he asks bluntly and, as much as I want to deny the accusation, I also want to feel him out. Is he really pissed or is he just doing his brotherly duty? And more importantly, would he mind if Alana and I dated for real?

Closing my truck door, I level with him. "If by messing around, you mean sleeping with her, no. And, to be honest, I wouldn't tell you if I were, because I don't disrespect women like that. But if you mean, am I seeing her, then yeah, I guess I am."

"She doesn't date bull riders," he snaps, and I cock my head to the side, curiously amused. I almost ask what the hell she has against bull riders, but I'm not about to give him the upper hand.

"No? Huh." I wink and leave it at that.

His jaw clenches a little tighter and I start to feel bad for the guy. I don't want to make him stroke out about something that might not ever progress beyond what we're doing now.

"Look," I begin, because I really don't want to piss him off or make him stroke out. "Wilder and I had this conversation earlier and I'm going to tell her what I do for a living. I know she won't tell anyone."

Aiden's gaze narrows. "Her telling anyone is the least of your concerns."

What the hell does that mean? "I'm seeing her this afternoon. I'll clear the air."

He glares for another long beat before his shoulders relax and a slow smile curls at one side of his mouth. "You do that. And then let me know how it goes."

Why do I get the impression he thinks I'm about to get my ass kicked?

Hell, maybe I am. But I can guaran-damn-tee that a five-foot-five, one-hundred-and-forty-pound woman ain't got nothing on a fifteen-hundred-pound bull with a cowboy on his back.

Then again, this is Alana Faulkner we're talking about.

# CHAPTER 11

ALANA

"*Y*ou're looking especially cheery today," Nancy says from behind the Mason Creek Market deli counter. Her long gray hair is pulled back in a braid and her red apron is as neat and clean as the moment she put it on this morning. Not because she doesn't work hard—she's a force to be reckoned with when it comes to her deli—but because she's just that tidy.

"It's a beautiful day and…" I glance down at my Fitbit. "We're both off the clock in an hour."

The older woman gives a small smile. "I am, but we both know you'll hang around for a few more."

"Nope, not today. I actually have plans for the afternoon that don't involve work or my classes."

She presses her hand to her chest in mock shock. "Well, I'll be darned. Alana Faulkner peeling herself away from this place…"

I laugh. "It's not that big of a deal."

"It's a huge deal," she counters. Then, "And I hope it's just the start of you doing it more often."

Me, too, but not so much that Marty starts to question my loyalties, now of all times. Hallie and I are meeting on Thursday to discuss my business plan and finance options and I'm crossing all of my available body parts that it goes well.

"By the way, I heard you have a new neighbor upstairs. He came yesterday for a sandwich, I assume before heading to the ranch." Nancy leans in toward the meat and cheese case, to keep whatever she's about to say between us and not the market-goers milling around behind me. "Don't tell my husband, but he's quite the looker. And he's got that, what are you kids calling it these days, swagger?"

A warm blush rises in my cheeks. "I, uh, I haven't noticed."

Her wide-eyed grin says she expects my nose to start growing or my pants burst into flames. "Uh huh."

I roll my eyes. "Anyway, I was hoping I could get you to throw some things together for me. Some sandwiches and a couple salads. Maybe pasta and the new vegetable medley. Oh, and if there's any cheesecake left, a couple slices of that, as well."

"Sure thing. Anything in particular you'd like on the sandwiches?"

"Um..." Crap. I have no idea what he likes, not that I get the impression he's picky. "Just whatever you put on Holden's yesterday, please."

Nancy's eyes darn near pop out of her head. "Girl, you'd better be telling me what I think you're telling me."

"I'm not saying anything." I laugh nervously, feeling a little like a giddy teenager while she makes a show of zipping her lips and throwing away the key. "It's not what you think it is."

"What isn't?" a familiar voice sounds behind me and I clench my eyes shut, every guilty muscle in my body tensing.

"Mom." I paste on a smile and slowly turn to face her. Let it be known that I love my mother to pieces and have no issues with her whatsoever. She, however, has issues with me, mostly stemming from the fact that I don't get out to the farm to see my parents nearly as often as I should. "Oh, my gosh, you cut your hair! I love it!"

She blinks at me, the rest of her expression blank. "Honey, I cut it a month ago."

Shit. "Oh. Um, has it really been that long?"

She makes a throaty sound and rolls her eyes much like I did to Nancy just a few moments earlier. In fact, I wouldn't doubt if it looked exactly the same, given Mom and I are virtual twins, save the twenty-five years between us.

"Is Dad here, too?" I ask, even though I know he isn't. Just like I'm always at the store, Dad is always working on the farm.

"No, he's tending to afternoon chores and smoking a brisket for dinner. You know, that thing we do every Sunday around five o'clock? It used to be a family thing, but…"

But Aiden moved to California and I went off to college and, even when I did come back to Mason Creek, I've rarely shown up, despite knowing how important this one simple thing is to my parents.

"Please come tonight, Alana. It would make your dad's day since he's cooking. He even made homemade coleslaw and potato salad." Her small, but hopeful smile is like a knife twisting slowly in my gut and, as much as I want to tell her I can't because I have plans with Holden, I can't bring myself to do it.

"Nancy, hold up on those sandwiches," I say over my shoulder, watching Mom's smile widen in my peripheral.

"You'll come?" she asks and I nod, the pretty pink

coloring her cheeks telling me it's the right decision. "Oh, honey, thank you so much!" She abandons her shopping cart to rush around and hug me and I find myself smiling, too.

"I assume Aiden and Emma are coming, too?"

"Yes. You know how much your brother loves brisket."

"I'm pretty sure there isn't a man alive who doesn't." I laugh and my thoughts go right back to Holden. Before I can think better of it, the question tumbles out. "Would it be okay if I brought a friend?"

Mom pulls back from the hug with wide eyes. "A boyfriend?"

"No." I laugh again, tucking a strand behind my ear with suddenly shaky fingers. Even though Holden and I aren't really dating, this feels an awful lot like bringing a guy home to meet the parents, something I've only done once before, with Cory. "He's just a friend, but he's in town for a few weeks and I'm sure he'd appreciate a home-cooked meal." Which sparks another idea altogether, but that's fodder for later, not now.

"Absolutely," Mom says, her hand curling around my arm. "You have no idea how happy this makes me, honey."

Actually, I think I do, and it's doing a hell of a number on my conscience right now. My excuse of needing to close up the store on Sundays expired a long time ago when I trained Susie and Peg to do it so I wouldn't have to all the time. Still, I chose to avoid time with my family, because so often it ended up reminding me of the past. A past I've come to realize maybe I've been holding on to, despite thinking I'd let go.

---

*How do **you feel about brisket?*** I text Holden an hour later when I get back upstairs to my apartment. Since I didn't have to pack for the picnic, I'd tried to stay a little longer, but Nancy dug her heels in and said she wouldn't leave unless I did, so I gave in.

He replies a few minutes later. *Fucking love it. Why? Is that what we're eating on our picnic?*

*About the picnic...* I hit send and bite my lip before shooting off the rest. *Would you mind having dinner at my parents' instead? Dad smoked a brisket today and he's sorta known around town for it.*

*My mouth is already watering, darlin.' Count me in.*

Thank god. Not that it would have been the end of the world if he said no, but then I'd be worried about what he was going to eat for dinner, because it dawned on me earlier that he's been living off of restaurant and bar food, save the sandwiches he gets from the market. I'm the least domestic person I know, but even I realize that's not good for anyone, never mind how expensive it must be.

*Thanks, Colorado. I owe you.*

*Owe me? Not even a little. See you soon.*

And I do. Less than an hour later, there's a knock on my door. I set my laptop aside and hurry across the apartment, pulling it open to a very sweaty, very sexy cowboy.

"Hi," I sigh, taking him in from head to toe and grinning at the mud covering his jeans. "I thought you said today was going to be a light day?"

"It was up until a feisty heifer got loose near the watering pond." He takes off his Stetson and swipes a lock of damp, dark blond hair from his forehead. "I hope I have time for a shower?"

"Yes, of course. We have about forty-five minutes."

He grins and a dimple pops in his cheek. "So, I'm meeting the parents, huh? Does this mean we're official now?"

God, he's adorable. "It means my mom caught me at the store today and reminded me that I'm long overdue for a visit. I couldn't say no, but I didn't want to leave you in the lurch either."

"Hey now, I'm a big boy. I can fend for myself."

"I may only be your fake love interest, but I can't keep letting you eat greasy diner and bar food."

He laughs. "You worried about me getting fat?"

"I'm worried about your arteries."

"Aww, darlin', that might be the sweetest thing you've ever said to me."

I tip my head to the side. "I'm nice sometimes."

A bark of laughter bursts from his chest. "And I thought the shit in the corral was deep."

"Stop." I shove at his shoulder. "You're giving me a complex."

His eyes dance back and forth between mine for a long moment, while a small smile settles on his lips. "You're not wearing any makeup," he finally says, his voice low, and instant heat fills my cheeks. Not the good kind.

"I need to get ready yet myself," I rush to explain. "I was doing homework and—"

"I love the freckles, darlin'. Whatever you gotta do to get ready, maybe don't cover these up." Holden reaches out and brushes his thumb across my cheekbone, and the self-conscious wave that just rose in my chest whooshes away in a heavy rush of relief.

This guy? He's got this fake date thing down pat.

HOLDEN

I haven't met the parents since I took Julia Denning to our senior prom. And back then, my eighteen-year-old self hadn't even thought twice about it. I hopped out of my truck, looked her daddy in the eye, and promised I'd get her back home by curfew, all the while knowing damn well I'd be *getting her off* at some point, too.

Alana and I aren't even a real thing. We've known each other a matter of days and I have no intention of getting handsy with her anytime soon. My dick might say otherwise, but my twenty-seven-year-old brain knows better. I like this girl. I like this girl a fucking lot and knowing I'm about to meet her folks has me feeling like I should have ten years ago…

Scared shitless.

Deciding I can't hide out in the bathroom forever, I open the door between the steamy room and her kitchen and holler, "Alana, you decent? Can I come in?"

"Yep! Just finishing my hair!" she calls back, probably from her bedroom, so I go inside, her sugary sweet perfume immediately hitting my nose and making my dick twitch.

*Don't even go there, dude. Not when we're about to shake her old man's hand.*

And then she saunters out of her room in a short navy sundress and no amount of scolding my cock is going to work. Friendly arrangement or not, he likes what he sees.

"Shit, darlin'," I mutter under my breath and a big grin splits across her face.

"You like it? I bought it forever ago and haven't had the chance to wear it yet. I figured my mom would at least be amused."

"Amused?" I can't stop looking at her. At the low neckline and all that creamy, freckled skin, at her bare legs that look just about perfect for wrapping around my waist.

"I'm not sure if you've noticed, but I'm not really a girly girl."

"The hell you aren't." She's kidding, right? I glance up to

see her purse her lips and tip her head to the side, like I'm blowing smoke. "I've seen all that frilly white bedding in your room, remember?" And I might've noticed a lacy bra or two in the bathroom hamper, as well.

"Okay, so maybe I have a slight girly side, but I don't really advertise it."

"One of your 'keep the men away' measures?"

She blinks.

"You forgot I already figured you out, huh?"

To that, she rolls her eyes and gives my shoulder a playful shove as she strides by. "You don't know everything about me, Colorado, so deflate that head a little bit."

I laugh. The head on my shoulders isn't really the one I'm concerned about right now.

She grabs a pair of sandals from by the door and then takes a seat in the kitchen to pull them on, muttering an almost inaudible, "Oh, and by the way, Aiden and Emma are coming, too."

Shit. I should have known there was a catch.

"I hope you don't mind?" She looks up at me, her teeth clasped around the corner of her bottom lip and I swallow down a groan.

"Nope. Not at all." It's not seeing Aiden I'm worried about, rather the conversation I promised him I'd have with her. A conversation I'm apparently going to have to start now rather than later.

"Oh, good. I was worried he might've actually shown up at the ranch today like you thought."

"Oh, he most certainly did."

Alana's mouth falls open and her hands still around the sandal straps she's trying to fasten. "Holden, I am so sorry."

"Nah, don't be." I take a seat on the arm of her couch and run a hand around the back of my neck. "But there's probably something we should talk about before we head out."

Her amber eyes lock on mine as she finishes with the shoe and places both hands on her knees. "Is this something my brother told you to do?"

"Yes, and he's right. You should know."

Her shoulders droop as she exhales a heavy sigh. "Just tell me you don't have a girlfriend or wife back in Colorado. That's all I really care about."

"I've never been married and I haven't had a girlfriend in years."

Relief eases her features. "Thank god."

"But that's not—"

She's on her feet with my face cupped in her hands before I can say another word. "I've already figured out you're the kind of guy I've sworn off. I'm even willing to bet you've ridden a bull or two."

I nod and swallow, and when I speak, my voice is hoarse. "Yeah, darlin', I have."

She pulls in a breath and strokes her thumbs over my cheeks, her eyes searching mine. "Then I guess we're both lucky that my apparent distaste for cowboys diminished at some point over the years, because I don't care."

"Maybe not, but—"

"Shh." She presses a fingertip to my lips. "You're here for a few weeks. This doesn't have to be complicated."

"This?" My hands lift to her hips and she bites that bottom lip again.

"Fake dating or not, I like spending time with you."

"I feel the same."

A soft smile tickles at her mouth. "Then nothing else matters."

# CHAPTER 12

ALANA

*I*'m pretty sure my dad is in love with Holden.

It might have something to do with the incessant comments about how amazing the brisket was, especially with Dad's homemade coleslaw on top, or it might've been Holden humoring Dad's rambling about all the time he spent in Colorado as a kid. Either way, Dad is smitten. Much to Aiden's dismay.

"Too bad he's not sticking around," my brother snarks as he joins me at the kitchen sink after Mom and Emma went to the barn to check on the baby goat that was just born yesterday.

"Dad isn't used to the company, that's all." I rinse off a plate and stick it in the drying rack.

Aiden leans against the counter and crosses one ankle over the other before taking a long pull from his beer. "He talk to you like I told him to?"

I shift a glare to my brother. "Yes, he did, but how about you tell me why you're really being an ass about me and

Holden?"

"Oh, I don't know, maybe because Cory—"

"Don't you dare bring him into this," I rasp, and Aiden's brows rise.

"Are you banging this guy? For real?"

*Smack!* I punch him in the bicep as hard as I can. "You know better than that!"

"Do I?" His eyes widen as he rubs at his arm. "Because he was in your apartment well before the sun came up, sis."

"For coffee, you Neanderthal. In case you didn't notice, the room you so generously hooked him up with isn't exactly fit for living."

"But you *did* go out with him last night. I saw you two making out on the sidewalk, remember?"

"Oh, my god." I press my fingers to my temples and close my eyes. "As grateful as I am that you're back in Mason Creek, sometimes I wish you were in L.A. again."

"What the hell does that mean?"

"It means that you're acting like an overbearing brute and for no good reason."

"I wouldn't say that. I—"

"Holden and I aren't dating. Not really. We just… we have an agreement."

Aiden's face pinches. "What?"

I blow out a breath and tug him a little deeper into the kitchen. "For one, keep your voice down. Two, I'm not going to explain this to you or try to justify it, because frankly it isn't any of your business. But trust me when I say you have nothing to worry about."

My brother lifts his chin as his jaw tightens. "I'm always going to worry about you."

"And I appreciate that, but this isn't one of those things you need to waste energy on. I promise."

"I don't like it."

"You don't have to like it, because this is my life, Aiden, not yours."

He narrows his eyes and opens his mouth to speak, but I cut him off.

"How about this? How about I promise that you're the first one I call if this ends up biting me in the ass? That way you can have the satisfaction of saying I told you so and kicking his ass at the same time?"

That finally, blessedly, makes him smile. "Now we're talking my language."

I roll my eyes. These small-town men are going to be the death of me.

---

WE SPEND the next couple of hours sitting on the front porch of my childhood home watching the sun go down.

Aiden and Emma skipped out shortly after she and Mom came back from the barn. My friend claimed the heat was getting to her, but from the way Aiden was doting on her every move, my guess is her ailment has nothing to do with the weather and everything to do with her and my brother making up for lost time in one of the most permanent ways possible.

While I'm happy as heck for them, I'd be lying if I said the realization that my best friend and my brother are not only in love but starting a family doesn't make me just the teensiest bit jealous.

I feel so behind in the game. So out of touch with how to even go about getting back on the field again. I know what Holden and I are doing is supposed to be helping me, but is it really? Because it seems to me that if I want to really do this... if I want to really start dating again so I can find someone to fall disgustingly in love with like Aiden and

Emma have, then I need to do this for real. Pretending and going through the motions might work for some, but I'm so out of practice that what we're doing isn't even scratching the surface.

And then there's the fact that I really do like Holden. He is exactly my type and, while I know there are things about him I don't know, I know enough to be sure those things don't matter.

I hinted as much earlier, which surprised even me. One minute, I was reminding myself that his compliments were just part of our deal and the next, I couldn't stop thinking about what it'd be like to say screw it and ask him out for real.

"You're quiet over there," Mom speaks up from across the small patio table between us. Dad and Holden are seated on the other side of the porch, engrossed in an intense conversation about ranch life.

"Just relaxing." I sigh and close my eyes as a blessed breeze dances across the porch, chilling my heated skin a half degree. "It's a great night for swimming."

"You should go." Mom's lighthearted, possibly even suggestive tone has my eyes snapping open again. She smiles. "He seems like a nice young man. Handsome, too."

Oh, god. "Mom…" I tried to be clear with both her and Dad that Holden is just a friend, but obviously I wasn't clear enough. "It's not like that. I know you've probably heard otherwise, but—"

"I'm not going by what I've heard—I'm going by what I've seen tonight."

And knowing my mother is one of the most perceptive people I know, I don't bother denying it. "I've only known him a few days."

"I fell for your dad the first time I set eyes on him."

My jaw drops. "Seriously?"

She nods, tucking a lock of auburn hair behind her ear. "Yep. In fact, we met at the Labor Day rodeo. He came with some friends from Colorado and never left."

Holy crap. "Why have you never told me this before?"

"You went from thinking boys were gross to being head over heels in love. And then when you weren't, you certainly weren't interested in hearing about other people's good fortune in relationships."

Ouch. Her words sting, but she isn't wrong. I hate that I pushed everyone away, but I'm hopeful that realizing it and acknowledging that it was my fault means I'm at least headed in the right direction to fix it.

"I'm sorry," I say quietly. Truthfully. Without any of the usual undeserving resentment. "I've been so selfish."

"Oh, honey, you were hurting. Sometimes we have to put up walls in order to protect ourselves and give our hearts time to heal. We just can't live like that forever." She reaches across the table and takes my hand as her words sink in, and I remember Holden saying something similar.

"I think I'm finally starting to realize that." I glance over her shoulder just as Holden looks up. Our eyes meet and a small smile plays on his lips. "If he's still in Mason Creek, do you mind if I bring him next week, too?"

Mom's eyes brighten. "I don't mind one bit, Alana Rose. Not as long as it means seeing you again."

Silly emotion brews in my chest as I stand and pull my mother up for a hug. We rock back and forth for what feels like forever before Dad clears his throat and demands a hug of his own.

"Don't be a stranger now, girly." His big hands rub up and down my back. "And be nice to this one, too." He thumbs over his shoulder. "He's a hell of a lot more personable than the last guy you brought home."

"Dad," I groan, and he laughs.

"Just giving you crap, sweet pea. Sort of."

Holden chuckles behind us, his dark eyes dancing in the porch light, as I thank my dad again for dinner and promise Mom I'll call in a couple days.

And then it's just me and Holden again, behind the closed doors of his truck.

"You survived," I say as soon as he turns the engine over.

"So did you." He winks across the cab as he backs around in the driveway. "Though for a second, I thought you might murder Aiden in the kitchen."

"Ugh, I don't want to talk about my brother. The rest of the night was so good." Easily the best visit I've had with my parents in forever, but then we haven't had many to compare it to. Something I fully intend to rectify.

"It was. Your old man is funny as hell and your mom... Good Lord, you two look alike."

I wrinkle up my nose. "Are you crushing on my mom?"

He laughs. "Darlin', you oughta know by now I only have eyes for you."

"Aww," I tease, but his words hit their mark, spreading a bit of warmth in my chest.

"If I'm honest, I'm not ready for the night to be over."

"No?" I ask, toying with the hem of my dress and trying to muster some courage. "How do you feel about getting wet?"

He flicks a raised eyebrow glance across the truck. "What?"

I press my lips into a smirk and shrug. "Just take a left at the stop sign."

HOLDEN

"This wetness you mentioned... It's not my blood, is it?" I kill the engine on the side of the road in the middle of nowhere and lean forward to peer out into the darkness.

Alana giggles, unbuckling her seat belt and popping open the passenger door. "Are you coming, Colorado, or are you too scared?"

Fuck, no, I'm not scared. I'm just... intrigued.

Climbing out, I click the truck locked and let Alana take my hand. She pulls me along the side of the road for a bit until she turns the flashlight on on her phone and lights up a narrow, but well-worn trail.

"You bring all of your fake boyfriends here?"

"Oh, my gosh, yes. All of them. You'll meet them in a minute. Well, their remains, anyway."

My bark of laughter echoes out into the night. "Great. You want my keys now, then? So you don't have to dig them from my pocket once you do me in?"

She giggles again and continues tugging me along the trail until a clearing comes into view. It's then that I spot the glisten of midnight blue water beyond the trees, lit up by a big silver moon.

"Ah. You drown them, huh?"

"It's not as messy and the fish appreciate the meal."

"Jesus Christ." I laugh, feeling her shaking shoulder nudge my arm as she laughs, too.

"For the record, this is Baylor Lake and there's a much more accessible beach on the other side of the old bridge in town. Unfortunately, there are probably still a few people there, in denial of their weekend coming to an end. I figured this is more private."

"Private? You plan on swimming?"

She nods. "I haven't been all summer and it was such a hot day. I thought we could take a dip. If that's okay?"

"Darlin', I'm never gonna turn down a nighttime dip with

a pretty girl." Though, it doesn't pass my notice that neither of us has a suit, and I'm curious as hell on how she plans to work around that.

She smiles up at me and then bends, making quick work of unfastening her sandals. "Just pretend my bra and panties are a bikini."

*Shittttt.*

"Don't be all weird about it, okay?"

Too late for that. I'm half hard just thinking about all that skin...

She kicks away her shoes and gestures impatiently for me to shed mine, as well. "Come on, Colorado. Don't be shy."

"What if I'm not wearing any underwear?"

She narrows her eyes. "Commando? I should have guessed."

Chuckling, I toe off my boots and socks, then reach behind my head to tug off my T-shirt.

Alana's gasp isn't nearly as discreet as I'm sure she hoped it would be and I grin.

"You all right, darlin'?"

"More than all right," she answers immediately, her fingers toying with the hem of her dress. "Just making sure you're not gonna get me half naked and then decide you're not going in."

"Oh, I'm going in." My belt buckle is undone in a second, followed by my fly, all the while my spunky little ice princess watches with fascination. "See something you like?"

She shifts slightly, the moon illuminating half of her face and the fact that she's biting her lip. In anticipation or is she second-guessing this idea of hers?

"And if I said I do?" she asks softly, her gaze sliding down my chest to my abs and lower, where my fingers have slowed to a snail's pace just to torment her like she's doing me.

"With no one around to hear you say it?" I cock my head

to the side and hook my thumbs in my waistband, watching a sly, almost wanton smile curve her lips. "Careful, gorgeous, or I might think you like me for real."

"Oh, that ego of yours." She laughs and I shake my head, because this girl? She's such a contradiction. Bold and full of sass one minute, timid and unsure of herself the next. But right now, she's the perfect mix of both. My little minx under the moonlight.

Motivated by her feisty attitude, I drop my jeans and hold my arms wide. "One of us is overdressed, woman."

She purses her lips. "Nice boxer briefs, you liar."

"Consider it a blessing, darlin', because if I was forced to go in naked, you would have been, too."

"Oh, really?" She cocks an eyebrow and, in one swift movement, lifts her dress over her head.

This time, I'm the one to gasp. Actually, it's more of a groan. A groan that rumbles all the way down to my balls.

She drops the dress on top of her sandals and takes off for the water in nothing but her bare feet and a minuscule bit of dark lace.

I'm right behind her, of course, because I'm pretty sure I'd follow her anywhere at this point.

"Holy shit, it's colder than I expected." Not that I'm complaining. It feels amazing, and frankly, my dick needs to cool off.

"It's perfect," Alana says, a little breathless as she dips low enough to cover her shoulders and wet her hair. "We used to come here all the time in high school. The public beach is nice, with picnic tables and whatnot, but we couldn't sneak beer and wine coolers over there."

I wade past her until the water hits my chest when I stand. "So, you were a rebel in high school, is that what you're telling me?"

"Nah, I was pretty normal. And it wasn't like we partied

every weekend. Most of us were athletes and getting caught would have been the end of that."

"Yeah? What'd you play?"

She glides closer, treading water to keep afloat less than two feet in front of me, as I dunk under to wet my head. "A little of everything," she says when I reemerge. "But softball was my sweet spot. How about you? Were you an athlete?"

"I'm not sure you want to hear about it." I spent my days on my uncle's ranch and my nights and weekends in the rodeo arena. And when I wasn't on a bull, aiming for those eight seconds, I was cheering on my buddies or watching the pros from the stands.

"The eternal cowboy, huh?" She shakes her head, but the light in her eyes holds no real condemnation. "I suppose we all have our faults."

"Oh, really?" I reach for her under the water, playfully digging my fingers into the soft sides of her stomach and making her squirm.

"Holden James!" she cries, twisting and turning and trying her damnedest to get away.

"James? Where the hell did you get that?" Laughing, I pull her back to my chest and pin one of her arms beneath mine while our free ones wrestle for control above the water.

She giggles and fights so hard, she can barely catch her breath, but the firecracker keeps trying.

"Made it... up," she wheezes, her fingers digging into my forearm, as if to inflict pain I barely feel. "Or maybe... it's... John Wayne."

I laugh so hard, I almost drop her. "Try again, darlin'. In fact, I'm not letting you go until you get it right."

"Rude!" she rasps, finally easing up enough to suck in a few lungfuls of air. "You don't play fair."

"You're the one who suggested we go swimming in our underwear, so don't get me started on fair."

She glances back, her breath still coming fast. "What's the big deal?"

"You think it was easy seeing you get damn near naked in front of me? Or the fact that we're practically skin on skin right now?"

Her eyes go wide. Then she challenges, "So put me down."

"And let you win? Fuck that." I chuckle, but the mood has already shifted. We stare at each other for a long moment before she whispers a single word...

"Daniel."

No friggin' way. "How did you know that?"

"Lucky guess," she says quietly and, though I'd just as soon keep her close to me all night long, I let go.

Only, she doesn't move.

At least not until she turns and lifts her hands to my chest as mine find her hips beneath the water.

"For the record, it wasn't easy seeing you get naked, either." Her hands slide up, stopping on my shoulders. "You're pretty hot for a cowboy."

A low laugh vibrates in my chest, while the thin bands of lace beneath my fingers tempt me into making this fake relationship we have very real.

"Are people who fake date allowed to kiss? Is that a thing?" I ask, boldly smoothing one hand down and around the fleshy curve of her ass.

"Do you want it to be a thing?" she rasps, her fingers sliding up and into my hair as she toes up and presses her tits against my chest as if to solidify her point.

I chuckle again. "What happened to the shy girl from the bar? The one who had no idea what she was doing to the men in this town?"

A brave smile curls her lips. "You're bringing her out of her shell."

"Am I?" Kinda hoping her bravery is reserved just for me,

though. And not for those other guys I'm supposed to be helping her attract. "Maybe she should kiss me so I can properly gauge the success of the experiment."

She smiles and her lips, all sure and confident, are on mine a second later. She half sighs, half moans as those fingers in my hair thread higher and I lift her so she can rest her elbows on my shoulders and bring our mouths even closer.

Fuck. I groan as her legs wrap around my waist. I've been hard since she whipped off her dress and there's no hiding that now.

"Holden," she sighs against my lips and I grip her tighter, refusing to break the kiss. I want to taste her. Consume her. Have as much of her as she'll let me have.

She parts her lips just slightly and it's an invitation I gladly accept, teasing my tongue against hers as the world fades away around us.

I like this girl. I like this girl so friggin' much. The little spitfire who wanted nothing to do with me is now the one driving *me* insane.

Beneath the water, she rotates her hips and presses her hot center against my swollen dick in a way that has my blood pumping even harder. She's the kind of girl I'd like to explore every inch of. Get to know every curve and every freckle before I make her mine. But if she wants me right here, right now in this lake, I won't deny her.

But she suddenly pulls away from the kiss, her breath coming hard and fast against my face. "We have to stop," she pants. "We... we can't."

"We can go home and—"

"No." She shakes her head and untangles herself from me before pushing back into the water. "I mean, we can't do *this*." She gestures between us, a mixture of longing and regret in her eyes before she spins and hurries out of the lake.

"Alana," I call after her, but she's already pulling on her dress and shoving her feet into her shoes.

Before I can even get out of the water, let alone tell her that we don't have to do anything at all, she's up the path and to my truck, slamming the door behind her.

## CHAPTER 13

ALANA

*I*t's been three days since I've talked to Holden. Not a single word or text since we parted ways in the hallway Sunday night after making out in the lake like a couple of horny teenagers.

Did I want to take things further with him? Of course, I did.

But did I want to do them the same way I'd done them with Cory all those years ago? I absolutely did not.

Holden may remind me of my ex in a lot of ways, but he's different, too. We may not know each other well, but he's already someone I'm never going to forget. When he's moved on from Mason Creek, I want my memories to be of him and only him.

I'm just not sure how to tell him that. That already this thing between us feels bigger than it was ever supposed to be.

But I have to try.

I have to, because something tells me that if I don't, I'll hate myself for it.

So, that's why I took off of work a little early and that's why I'm currently setting a thermal bag holding a small pan of lasagna and some garlic bread outside of his door.

I probably should have just invited him over like a big girl, but I haven't been the only one to go radio silent these past few days. He hasn't tried to reach out, either. Hasn't come by for morning coffee or knocked to let me know he's home in the evening. If it's because he's realized I'm too much of a head case, I don't want to hear it in his voice when he turns me down.

I pad back into my apartment and to my laptop, where I've been scouring over my business plan in between cooking. My meeting with Hallie is tomorrow and I don't want to look like a complete amateur, even if I know she won't judge me for it.

My phone chirps with a text and my breath hitches in my throat when Holden's name appears on the screen.

**Heading upstairs. Can we talk?**

Speak of the devil. My thumbs hover above the keyboard, but I can't bring myself to respond. I just left food outside of his door like some sappy girl trying to win her man back.

That isn't me.

Or at least, it hasn't been me in such a long time and—

**Did you cook for me?**

Um…

*Knock knock.*

Oh god.

I jump up from the couch and rush to my room to run a brush through my hair and make sure I don't look like hell, because, yep, I've definitely become *that girl.*

"Hey," I say when I finally open the door to the very handsome, very sexy cowboy leaning against the wall with my thermal bag hanging from his fingers.

"You made me lasagna," he says easily, his dark gaze locking on mine.

"Uh, yeah. I figured you must be tired of grabbing dinner out by now."

His lips hitch to one side. "Want to share it with me?"

That hadn't been my plan, but… "Sure." I step aside and wave him in.

"It smells amazing," he says as he sets the bag on the table and unzips. "Garlic bread, too? Damn."

Heat fills my cheeks as I grab two plates from the cupboard and utensils from the drawer. "I know you like Italian, so I figured it was a safe bet."

"Darlin', anything you cook for me is a safe bet."

When I turn back around, he's right there, leaning down to peck my cheek.

"Thank you," he says softly, one hand lifting to my hip.

"It's not a big deal." Even if it is the first time I've ever cooked for a man.

"It is when I've spent the past few days thinking you might never talk to me again."

"Holden—"

"Look, I know this isn't supposed to be real, but fuck if it doesn't feel like it's exactly that." His eyes dart back and forth between mine. "I know I'm not the kind of guy you want—"

"You're exactly what I want." The confession tumbles past my lips before I can stop it, and the relief on his face makes my chest ache.

"Darlin'…" He takes the plates and forks from me and sets them on the counter, before wrapping me up in his big arms. "Fuck, I've missed you."

"I've missed you, too," I say against his stubbled jaw when

he buries his face in my neck. "And that scares the crap out of me."

He presses his nose to the soft spot behind my ear and inhales. "I know, babe."

"I'm just… I'm afraid of liking you too much, you know? You'll be leaving soon and I haven't done this in so long and—"

"Shh." He pulls back and cups my face in his big, calloused hands. "It scares me, too, but I'm already invested, darlin'. I'm already so fucking wrapped up in you that it's hard to think about anything else."

"Really?" I swallow hard and wet my lips as he nods.

"Yeah. But I don't want to rush you into something you're not ready for, either." His thumbs stroke over my cheeks. "We can do this however you want to do it as long as I don't have to go another three days without talking to you."

"A week ago, you didn't even know me."

"Which is total bullshit. So glad I remedied that."

I smile and toe up to press a quick kiss to his lips. "Me, too."

He groans at the connection but forces himself to step back and not take it further. "We'd better eat, darlin'."

So, we do. For the next hour, we eat and talk, and his company is a fast reminder that I don't want to go back to living as a loner again. Chatting with customers in the store is nice, but sitting down and having a conversation with someone is so much better. Then again, there's a good chance I feel this way because it's Holden I'm conversing with.

"So, do you think Old Man Morton will hold off putting the store up for sale until you figure out your finances?" Holden asks as he stretches his legs out on the floor near the coffee table where we ate.

"Probably not. He's already been waiting a while."

"Surely a little longer isn't going to hurt him."

"He's going to be seventy-seven in a few months. And he doesn't have any family, aside from a nephew in Idaho. It's not like there will be anyone to step in and take care of things if something happens to him."

"Shit, that sucks." Holden tips back a hefty gulp of water. "Do you have any idea how much the place is worth?"

"Unfortunately, yes."

"Unfortunately?"

"It's about ten times my annual salary."

He nods, a thoughtful look on his face. "That's actually not a horrible ratio."

"When you have little to nothing for a down payment, it's terrifying."

"I'm sure Hallie will talk you through all of the options. And I bet Marty would help you out with the down payment, too. Maybe advance it to you as part of the selling price. People do it all the time when they're buying a house."

I'd thought of that, too, but wanted to see what Hallie had to say before I approached the subject with Marty.

"You said you changed majors to business, right? What was your major before that?"

"Public relations."

His eyebrows rise. "You wanted to be a publicist?"

I nod. "Yep. And as much as I hated wasting so many credits, it worked out for the best. I don't think I would have been happy in PR."

"No? I think you would've rocked it. No way you'd take any shit from the press when they do your clients wrong."

Providing my clients weren't lying, cheating assholes like Cory turned out to be.

"Would have loved to have you on my side with the assault accusations, but instead..." His brow creases as he shakes his head. "Guess there's no point in wishful thinking. It is what it is."

"I'm sorry." I can tell it eats at him. Every now and again, he gets this distant look in his eye and I know he's thinking about it. "So, you said your boss wanted you to take some time away. Does he have a set date in mind for your return or are you playing it by ear?"

He lifts a shoulder. "Not sure. Haven't talked to him in a few days."

"You will go back, though, right?"

His gaze shifts to his jeans where he picks at something nonexistent. "I don't know. I'm not sure if I can keep working for people who don't want to support me."

His disappointment is palpable. But it runs deeper than that. He's hurt, too. His boss—this ranch he worked for—it meant something to him and it's killing him, knowing he didn't mean as much to them.

"I'm gonna take a shower." He gets to his feet, the crease in his brow deep as he looks everywhere but at me. "I'll come back and help you clean up when I'm done," he mutters, taking his plate and empty water bottle to the kitchen.

"That's okay. I've got it." I follow after, hating the pain radiating off of him. I reach out to touch his arm, but he moves away before my fingers connect. I'm not sure it was intentional, but I'm not confident it wasn't either.

"Thanks, Alana. For dinner and for…" He shoves his hands into his pockets restlessly. "For everything, I guess."

Um, why does it sound like he's pushing me away when an hour earlier he was telling me he wanted to keep doing whatever it is we're doing?

"You're welcome." My voice cracks and I bite my lip as he heads for the door, his only goodbye a quick dip of his chin before he ducks out.

The door latches shut behind him and suddenly I wonder

if there's more to his story than he's said. If maybe he was trying to tell me that the other day before we left for my parents'.

Maybe he'd needed to talk, but I shut him down because I'd been so concerned that his truth wouldn't be something I'd want to hear.

God, I'm selfish.

This man has done nothing but do what he can to help me since he's come to town and I wouldn't even hear him out when he tried to talk to me. No wonder he doesn't want to say more now.

I make quick work of cleaning up the kitchen and escape to my bedroom before I even hear the shower turn on.

I already know what I have to do. What I want to do. I just need to bide my time and leave him alone with his thoughts for a bit.

I open my laptop, clicking away from the article I'd been reading for one of my classes, and bring up Google instead.

The urge to do as I told him I wouldn't—to look him up and find out more—is strong. But I can't make myself enter his name. I can't break his trust like that. If he wants me to know, then he should be the one to tell me. I just need to give him the chance.

I sit on the bed, reading, but not comprehending, the article for almost an hour before I can't take it anymore. I can't let him stew over this and let his emotions fester any longer.

I head to the kitchen and the scent of his body wash hits me like a comforting blanket, making me close my eyes for a moment and sigh beneath its warmth.

The shower isn't running and there's silence on the other side of the bathroom door, so I push inside to freshen up before I go to his door for the second time today.

My gasp registers in my ears before my brain fully

acknowledges that, despite the silence, my bathroom is not unoccupied.

In fact, it's very occupied. By a very naked, very hard Holden.

"Oh god, I'm so sorry." I slap a hand over my eyes, but it's pointless. The image of his lean, muscled body is already etched in my mind. His broad shoulders, his defined chest, the trail of light brown hair from his belly button all the way down to his insanely gorgeous cock. "It was so quiet, I assumed you were finished."

He doesn't say a word and from what I can tell, doesn't move either. He's quiet for so long that I peek through my fingers, wondering if maybe I'd imagined him. But nope. NOPE.

Not only is he still very real, but he's staring at me, those dark, stormy eyes narrowed as he wraps a hand around his erection and, sweet mother, *strokes* himself.

My hand falls away from my face as my mouth slacks open and I stare.

*Stare* at that big hand slowly and torturously sliding up and down his length.

"Holden…" I exhale his name, my voice barely a whisper as my heart begins to race and the room begins to spin, yet I. Can't. Look. Away.

He continues to touch himself, his chin lowering while the storm in his eyes turns predatory. Dangerous even, and it sends goose bumps across my skin.

If he were another man, I might be afraid.

Hell, if he were another man, I would've turned and fled immediately.

But he isn't. And I'm not. And I won't.

Because something tells me he needs me as much as I need him.

# CHAPTER 14

HOLDEN

"*H*olden..." She sighs and her pretty lashes lower over hazy amber eyes.

I should have reached for a towel or, at the very least, turned away to spare her any further embarrassment.

But I couldn't.

Not when I realized she could have just as easily turned away, too.

Her gaze drops to my fist once again, and her chest begins to rise and fall a little faster with every passing second. Even though she's wearing a bra beneath her T-shirt, I can still see the pebbled peaks of her nipples poking through the lace.

She likes what she sees.

It's all I can do not to take the three steps between us and pick up where we left off on Sunday night. I can see her desire for me as clearly in her eyes now as I could feel it in her body at the lake, but she needs to be the one to take us over that line. She needs to be the one to decide how we spend our next few weeks together.

I drop my chin when the ache in my balls begin to build and I can't help but stroke harder. My hand slides up and down my shaft, circling over the crown, and squeezing at the base.

I need to come, but I don't want to do it like this. Not unless that's what she wants.

"Darlin'," I mutter through clenched teeth. "I'm about to embarrass myself, so if that's not something you want to witness, I suggest you head back into your apartment."

Nostrils flaring, her eyes flick to mine before the tip of her tongue dips out to trace her lips. "Do I have other options?" she pants.

A low chuckle rumbles in my chest. "Sweetheart, don't play with me."

The slender column of her throat works as she swallows… and then she steps forward. "What if that's what I want? To play?"

Jesus Christ. "Darlin', I'm about thirty seconds away—"

She closes the distance between us and presses her tits to my chest, her hot breath pulsing against my throat. Her hands lift to my arms and her fingers flex into my skin as she tips her head back and her eyes lock on mine.

"Let me," she whispers, but instead of swapping my hand for hers, she drops to her knees instead. In less time than it takes my brain to catch up and realize what she's doing, her lips wrap around my dick.

"Alana…" My hands thread through her hair, my intent to stop her, but she only opens wider and takes me back farther. "Baby, you don't have to do this."

She blinks up at me and pulls back, gripping the base of my dick while she swirls her hot, wet tongue around the tip.

The look in her eyes is a mix of lust and determination and when she sucks me so deep that her eyes water, there's nothing I can do but hold on and enjoy the ride.

"Oh shit, I'm gonna come," I warn her, my trembling hand gentling in her hair as the telltale flare of impending release ignites in my balls.

But my pretty Montana ice princess doesn't let up. She opens wider instead, swallowing every bit of me as I go over the edge.

"Jesus Christ," I mutter when my vision finally comes into focus again and Alana's sexy, satisfied smile shines up at me. "Come here," I growl, hauling her to her feet so I can kiss the hell out of her.

She laughs against my lips, not bothering to stop me when I tug her T-shirt off and push her leggings down to the floor.

"You know what you just started?" I rasp.

"Me?" Her eyes go wide as she giggles. "Pretty sure you're the one who did that."

Yeah, maybe I did, but she sure as hell had no problem jumping in. "Better cancel your plans for tonight."

"Oh?" Her eyebrows lift as I spin her around and smack her ass.

"This cowboy isn't anywhere near done with you yet."

ALANA

Holden cranks the shower on again and has us beneath the spray in seconds.

"And here I thought you were a good girl," he murmurs, sweeping my hair to the side as he leans in from behind and kisses my neck. "But you have a dirty side, don't you?"

The combination of his words and his touch sets my nerves on fire and I squirm, my ass pressing back into his lap.

"How are you hard again?" I gasp, and he chuckles against my ear.

"All you, babe. You've been driving me crazy since the second you opened your door and shot those ice daggers at me."

My laugh morphs into a moan as his hand glides from my waist to one of my breasts.

"You're perfect," he whispers, his fingers gently tweaking my aching nipple. "So full of fire and so fucking beautiful."

My head falls back against his shoulder as he continues to play, his tender, but intentional ministrations tightening the cord of desire running between my breasts and clit.

"Holden…" I groan, already so desperate for him to take this further. To touch me like I know we both want him to.

"You like that?" he asks softly, his free hand lifting to my other breast as stars light up behind my eyes. I whimper and he begins to tug and tweak in tandem until my knees shake. "Shit, you're sensitive. Turn around for me."

In a dazed cloud of lust, I do as he says and am rewarded with the dip of his head and the heat of his tongue replacing his fingers.

"Oh god!" I cry and grip his hair. Is it possible to come from nipple play alone? Because if he keeps this up…

"So pretty," he praises, his lips teasing against one bud and then the other, licking and sucking until my pussy pulses with greedy need.

"Touch me," I beg, and his hand is between my thighs in an instant.

"I want to taste you, darlin'. Want your sweetness on my tongue." His fingers slide between my folds and my entire body hums. I want that, too, but I've never… Rather, no one's ever…

He lowers to a squat in front of me, the hot spray of the shower raining down around us, and I think I might die from the sight of him before me, parting me with his thumbs.

"Fucking hell," he murmurs, his eyes darkening as he takes me in. "You're so goddamn beautiful."

A heated blush seeps into my cheeks and I close my eyes.

"Not a chance, darlin'. Open those pretty eyes for me. Watch as I make you come."

Oh. My. God.

He lifts one of my legs and places it over his shoulder before he's. Right. There. His tongue, his lips, his nose. Licking, sucking, nudging while my ears begin to ring.

And then he pushes a finger inside. Then two. Pumping in and out while he devours me.

"Holden, oh god…" I've never felt like this before. Never felt so many sensations at once. Never felt so utterly worshiped by a man.

I open my mouth to tell him, but my orgasm comes out of nowhere and I cry out instead, my fingers gripping his hair. "Oh my god, oh shit, *Holdennnn*!"

He holds me close, placing soft, languid kisses on my thighs, until the last wave of my release ebbs away and the buzz in my ears fades.

"You okay?" He stands and pulls me into his chest with his arms around my shoulders.

All I can do is nod, press my cheek to his chest, and close my eyes.

It may have been a while since a man has touched me, but I am absolutely certain it never felt like that.

"Let's wash up quick and talk some more."

"Talk?" I ask, my voice hoarse. He's still hard against my stomach and I'd really like to know if he's as talented with that appendage as he is with his fingers and tongue.

He chuckles into my hair. "For starters."

Thank god.

HOLDEN

Alana tucks her hands between her cheek and a pillow and watches as I discard the towel and slide into the bed beside her.

"So…" A small smile plays on her lips as I pull her naked body against mine. "Things have taken an interesting turn, haven't they?"

I smooth a damp lock of hair back behind her ear. "I can't say I'm surprised. You?"

"I think I knew. I mean, obviously I fought it at first, but I knew."

"I was just that tempting, huh?"

She laughs and shoves at my chest. "You are so full of yourself, Colorado."

"Mmm…" I lean in and bury my face in the curve between her neck and shoulder, inhaling her vanilla sugar scent. "I'm hoping *you'll* be full of me soon, too."

"Holden Daniel," she groans. "I thought you wanted to talk."

"We are talking, gorgeous."

"No—you're seducing me."

"'Seducing' as opposed to 'trying to seduce' implies it's working, babe." I nip at her earlobe and am rewarded with the sweetest shudder. "See that? Your body is definitely more interested in something other than talking."

"Unghh." She falls onto her back in defeat and I quickly roll over, covering her bare skin with my own.

"You are such a contradiction." I dip for a kiss, but she turns her head.

"What do you mean?"

Nudging one knee between her legs, she opens without

hesitation and I grin. "That right there. You fight me one minute, but give in the next. I fucking love it."

"Are you saying I'm weak?" She narrows her eyes, but there's no spite in them. Just desire I'm more than happy to oblige.

"Weak for me maybe."

She rolls her eyes and I chuckle.

"You keep proving my point, darlin'. And for the record, there's nothing wrong with being weak for your man. As long as he's the only one you're weak for."

"My man?" Her lips twist into a smirk, but her breathy voice gives her away. And this time when I lower for a kiss, she doesn't stop me.

In a matter of minutes, the exchange becomes fervid. All tongue and roaming hands and her soft, pliant body moving beneath mine.

"Holden," she rasps my name again, which is easily becoming my favorite sound. "I want you."

"Yeah?" My lips move to her jaw and her neck, then her collarbone and below, until they close around one perfect, pink nipple.

"Ohh…" Her low groan, followed by the scrape of her fingernails down my back as she arches hers, is pure octane for my already throbbing dick.

Twisting my hips, I wedge even deeper between her thighs until her slick, wet heat welcomes me.

"You want me like this?" I rasp, rocking against her in a slow, torturous rhythm that coats my dick with her wetness without slipping inside.

"More," she pleads, her body bucking beneath mine. "There are condoms in the nightstand. Please."

*My fucking pleasure.*

I lean over and fumble through the drawer until I find a strip of foil packets and quickly take care of business.

"You sure, beautiful?" I whisper, notching back into place with my elbows on either side of her head. "Look at me and tell me."

Her whiskey eyes flutter open and the desire she shares with me is unlike anything I've seen before. I want to slam in and claim her. Wrap myself up in her and never leave. But I need to hear her say it first.

"I feel like I've waited my entire life for this," she whispers, and while the depth of her confession should give me pause, it only fuels me. I have no idea what will happen with us when it's time for me to go, but right now, I don't care. "I'm sure, Holden. Please."

It's all I need.

I slick my cock through her folds and push inside, inch by glorious inch, as she watches me fill her until there's nothing between us.

"Oh god," she murmurs, flicking her gaze from mine to our joined bodies and back again. "Look at us, Holden."

Yeah. I see it too. Utter friggin' perfection that would have never happened if it hadn't been for my fucked-up life.

I don't want to move, because I don't want this to be over. But I also want to fuck myself so far into her, mind, body, and soul, that she never forgets me.

So I move. And I do my damnedest to make her feel as much of me as she can, as deep inside of her as is humanly possible, because I want her to know that in a matter of a week, she's made her way inside of me, too.

I never wanted to come to Montana, but I already know that when my time is up, I'm not going to want to leave, either.

# CHAPTER 15

ALANA

*H*olden's stayed over for the past two nights and I'm fairly certain his occupancy of the little room across the hall is over.

Ten days.

He's been in my life for ten days and I already dread the morning I wake up alone.

Thank god that day isn't today.

I press a kiss to his chest and trail my fingers up and down the smooth, muscled ridge of his abs, teasing a little lower to where his erection tents the sheet. His alarm will go off in ten minutes, but I'm confident he'd rather wake up to my touch than the annoying beep of his phone.

"Mmm, good morning to you, too," he murmurs, his voice husky from sleep.

"I'm sorry. He looked like he wanted attention."

He chuckles. "He always wants your attention, babe. Unfortunately, I have to be up in five minutes or Wilder's gonna have my ass."

"Ugh. Damn Wilder."

Holden presses a kiss to the top of my head. "What time are you meeting with Hallie today?"

"Three. Susie is coming in early to cover for me." Hallie and I met yesterday, too, but she ended up having to sit in for Brayden at a last minute bank meeting, so we didn't get to finish running numbers. "I can't believe she liked my business plan."

"Well, of course, she did. You're a genius."

"You haven't even seen it." I poke at his side and he chuckles.

"I don't need to see it to know you killed it, babe." He rolls so we're face to face. "But I wouldn't mind seeing it some-time. You know, if you wanted to show me."

"Really?" I pull back in surprise. "You'd be interested in something like that?"

He frowns. "Yeah, darlin'. I'm interested in you, so by association, I'm interested in what you want to accomplish."

My silly heart clenches and I press my lips to his in a hard kiss. "You can't say things like that to me when we both need to get out of this bed."

His fingers dig into my hip as he deepens the kiss for just a moment before breaking away. "If we didn't need to be in Rebel River by seven o'clock, I'd show you just how inter-ested I am."

"Rebel River again?" He mentioned helping a friend of Wilder's over the weekend, but I assumed it was a one-time thing.

"Yup. I guess Sandy wants to try a new feeding system for the cattle and she wants to run it by Wilder before she brings it up with the foreman. He's been giving her a lot of hassle and I think she's trying to avoid the conflict."

"The Magnolia Blue Ranch? Isn't that the one right along the river?"

"Yup. Friggin' gorgeous. Not a ton of land, but it's a hell of a setup."

His eyes light up as he talks about the place, which is something I've noticed a lot lately when he talks about working on Wilder's ranch. That shine, however, doesn't seem to be there when he talks about his job back in Colorado.

His phone begins to chime from the nightstand and he groans as he rolls over to shut it off. "One of these days, we're going to sleep in and not get out of bed until noon."

I laugh. "Uh huh, sure." I've opened the market all but two days in the past four years and I don't see that changing anytime soon.

"A guy can dream, right?" He twists to give me another quick kiss before crawling out of bed. "You're not heading back to work after meeting with Hallie, are you?"

"Ugh, I should. Then again, Susie's working tonight and she can close up, too. Why?"

He flashes a mischievous grin. "Was hoping I could take you out tonight."

I fake gasp and press a hand to my chest. "Like a date?"

He dips his chin. "Yes, ma'am. And none of that pretend shit."

I giggle, knowing damn well that we were never really fake dating. There was always something very real about it, even though we tried to pretend otherwise.

"And how exactly will this real date differ from a pretend date?" I ask, curiosity rising as I reluctantly slide from the bed, as well.

But Holden merely shakes his head, a crooked grin turning up one side of his mouth. "Nope, darlin'. You're not getting any hints from me. Just wear something pretty and be ready at six."

"Something pretty, huh?" Padding around the bed in my bare feet, I toe up to steal a kiss. "I'll see what I can do."

HOLDEN

"Sometimes I think I should just sell the place," Sandy says with a defeated sigh as her fingers worry the corner of the coaster beneath her glass of iced tea.

Wilder and I had arrived early and had spent all morning walking the ranch with her, helping her make a list of all the things that needed updating. While there wasn't much—Dean had actually done a pretty good job on the upkeep—what we did find seemed to cause her more and more stress.

And that was the thing about owning and running an operation like this. You either had it in you or you didn't. Sandy had busied herself with raising a family and maintaining the domestic side of the ranch, while her husband handled the rest. Now that she was in charge of it, the truth was slowly revealing itself. This wasn't how she wanted to spend the rest of her life.

"Dean's mentioned taking over and maybe even buying the ranch someday, but I don't think he has the means to do so. At least not within the next ten years and I don't know that I want to wait around, knowing I'm still responsible for all of this in the meantime, whether he's running everything or not." She adjusts in her seat, the legs of the chair screeching slightly against the hardwood floor beneath the oversized dining table. A table that I imagine sits most, if not all of the ranch hands, a few times a week.

"I know you two butt heads more than is good for either of you, but I do think he means well, San." Wilder passes her a small smile. "In fact, he's probably feeling the same kind of pressure you are, to keep the Magnolia Blue running just like Hank did."

The older woman nods. "I know. And part of me wants to give him a chance, but I'd have to do so at my own expense and I just... I don't know that I have it in me." When she glances toward the big bay of windows and the rolling fields that lead to the Rebel River, the glisten of emotion in her eyes is unmistakable. "I want to sell. Ideally to someone who will keep my crew at work and make sure their families are fed. Hank would want it that way."

I don't know this woman well, but something propels me to reach across the table and cover her hand with mine. "I can tell this is weighing heavily on you, and while I never knew Hank, I think he'd want you to be happy, too."

A flash of emotion dances across her face and her bottom lip begins to quiver as she turns her hand over beneath mine and squeezes. "I want to do right by him more than anything else," she whispers.

"We know you do," Wilder says. "And I did know Hank, so I can confidently say that if selling is what you want, then he would support you in that decision."

She lets go of my hand to swipe her tears. "My daughter Sarah said the same. In fact, she's already talking about moving me into her guest house, so I can be close to my grandbabies."

I chuckle. "Well, that sounds just about perfect."

"Sarah lives in California," Wilder says with a scowl as if the Golden State is anything but.

"I don't care if it's downtown L.A., as long as I can see my babies more." Sandy glances back and forth between us, a smile slowly replacing the fear and unease. "Thank you both for this. For just listening and hearing me out."

"You know I'm here for you, Sandy. Anything you need, just ask."

She tucks a strand of gray hair behind her ear and bites her lip. "Would you... would you be here when I have Grady or Cole come out to look things over?"

Wilder dips his chin. "Absolutely."

Her relief seems to lighten her shoulders and it puts me at ease, too. Again, I don't really know Sandy and I never had the pleasure of meeting her late husband, but I felt a connection to this woman and to this ranch the moment I stepped out of the truck last week. Wilder's ranch has a similar vibe. Both are more than a business and a means of livelihood. They exude a feeling of family. Of connection and stability and the promise for a future built on something solid.

Wilder turns his truck into the long driveway of the Roman Wilde Ranch an hour later, the trip from Rebel River back to Mason Creek filled with idle chitchat about what will come next for Sandy.

Wilder offered to be there as a token of moral support when she talked to her staff, but she declined, claiming it would be too emotional and she didn't want to burden him that way when he'd already done so much. She could handle that part of things if he'd help her with the realtor to ensure she gets a fair price.

"You're thinking about it, aren't you?" he asks when he puts the truck into park in front of the stable.

"Thinking about what?" I frown like I don't know exactly what he's talking about and he smirks.

"You won the world title a couple years back. You've got a boatload of money sitting in the bank, am I right?"

I give a low laugh, my newfound bitterness for ABR rearing its ugly head. "I have money in the bank because I've invested it, not only because of the friggin' ABR."

He cants his head in acknowledgment, then, "You know that's not what I'm really asking."

Yeah, I do, but I'm not sure of more than that right now.

Of course, I'd love a place like Magnolia Blue. In fact, it's no secret I've wanted a ranch of my own someday. My dream has always been to retire from bull riding and get back to my roots. Back to work that provides far more than entertainment. To work that means something.

Magnolia Blue is the perfect setup. It's not too big. It's friggin' beautiful. And it would come with a legacy, too. A history of Sandy and Hank's hard work and Hank's family before them. Something I could help them carry on.

I didn't come here looking, but I'd be a fool not to seriously consider Magnolia. After all, what are the chances the perfect opportunity would present itself while I was here?

I don't know what will happen with the ABR, but then… does the decision have to be theirs? If I want this—this chance for a new career and a future right here in Montana —then maybe I should be the one to make the next move.

ALANA

"We may have a problem with capital," Hallie says, her lips twisting thoughtfully as she reviews the computer screen.

Even though I knew as much, my stomach still sinks. "What kind of number are we talking about?"

She lifts a shoulder. "Depends on the final appraisal of the store and an in-depth review of the market's financials. Do you think Marty would allow me to take a look?"

"I don't see why not. He knows you're helping me, and I

honestly believe he wants me to be the one who buys the store."

She nods and then hesitates. "I know it might be difficult, but you may want to have a conversation with him about the down payment. We could get creative and ultimately have him front the money."

I pull in a deep breath and rub my fingers nervously against my jeans. "Holden mentioned that, too." And I have a feeling Marty would do what he could to help me out. But another part of me worries that Marty may not be around long enough for me to pay him back. That doesn't feel right.

"Speaking of which…" Hallie spins away from her computer and levels a curious glance my way. "What in the heck is going on with you two?"

"Who? Me and Holden?" I ask, knowing darn well I'm only delaying the inevitable by a few moments.

She cocks her head to the side. "Really? We're going to do this?"

I laugh and glance toward the windows as warmth fills my cheeks. An older couple strolls past on the sidewalk, and my nervous laughter melts into longing.

"He's helping me out with something," I say. Or rather he was, but now…

"What kind of something?" Hallie persists, and I turn back to her with a sigh. I've never been good at lying, and right now I'm not sure I even want to.

"Actually, he was helping me, but we've sort of flipped the script."

Her perfect brows lift. "Oh, I think I like where this is going. Go on."

Sucking in a deep breath, I tell her everything. Well, everything but the sleeping together bits. She can put those pieces together herself if she wants to.

"Let me get this straight," she says, flattening her hands on her desk and leaning in a bit. "He offered to go out with you to get the other guys in town talking and even more interested, but now you're really dating?"

I tip my head back and forth, then nod. "More or less. Except when we were faking it, we wanted everyone to think it was real. And now that it's real, we don't want anyone to know."

She blinks at me.

"I told Aiden we had an arrangement, which at the time was true. Now that it's real, I'd really like him to continue thinking it's nothing he needs to worry about."

"Ah." Her smirk turns into a light laugh. "I can understand that."

"He tries to make up for lost time or something with the overprotective big brother act. Wilder probably told you he showed up at the ranch over the weekend to give Holden hell."

"Yeah, he mentioned it. He also said you haven't dated in a while."

My gaze flicks to hers. "Wilder said that?"

She nods, then in a low voice adds, "You must really like him."

Butterflies lift in my stomach and I don't bother to deny it. "I do. And that's crazy, isn't it? He's only been here ten days."

Her smile widens and then she shakes her head. "Wow."

"What? Why are you looking at me like that?"

"Either you're more out of practice than I realized and you genuinely think it's weird to connect with someone you've just met or your feelings for him already go beyond *like*."

"Oh." The back of my neck begins to burn and the fluttering in my belly grows. "A little of both maybe?"

Hallie makes a soft throaty sound. "Maybe leaning a little more towards the latter?"

I swallow hard because admitting that to someone else when I've barely accepted it myself stirs up both relief and fear. I finally told Madelyn about Holden, but she's been too busy to have any significant conversation. And I could never tell Emma for fear she'd tell Aiden.

But also admitting that Holden is the kind of guy I could easily get serious about is terrifying. He'll leave Mason Creek soon, and there's no doubt he's already going to take a piece of me with him.

Maybe it was the timing of my life and my readiness to pull out of my funk… or maybe it was meeting Holden that set it all into motion, I don't know. But I do know that he's special and in the short time he's been in my life, he's already left his mark.

# CHAPTER 16

HOLDEN

*I* haven't planned a date like this in... well, forever. Not that I haven't dated plenty of women over the years, but because I haven't wanted to impress one as much as I do Alana.

Obviously, I like her, but there's an urgency to this thing between us, too. The clock is ticking and I want to make our time together as memorable as possible. I want to be a guy she never forgets. Or more accurately—*the* guy she doesn't *want* to forget.

After a secret exchange with Hallie and a few stops around town, I get everything situated in my truck and then head upstairs to pick up my girl.

I rub my sweaty palms against my jeans and take a couple of deep breaths before raising my hand to knock. But the door opens before I get a chance and the composure I'd just tried to collect flies out the window.

"Holy shit," I stammer, and Alana simply smiles before turning in a full circle before me. She's wearing a white dress with tiny pink flowers and enough cleavage to make my mouth water. The dress lifts from her thighs as she spins and it's a damn good thing we're going to be alone, because I'm not about to share all of this skin with anyone else.

"Another dress I found in my closet with the tags still attached," she says with a sigh, and I gulp.

"You got any more hidden away? Because I'll gladly plan a date for every single one of them if it means you'll wear them for me."

She giggles and rolls her eyes, but I'm dead fucking serious. Not only has this girl deprived herself of having fun for far too long, but the idea of her sharing this side of herself with anyone else pisses me off. I want all of it. All of her. For me and only me.

"Do I need anything else?" she asks, draping her purse over her shoulder. "A sweater maybe?"

I shake my head. "Nope. You don't need a thing."

She narrows her eyes, a curious smile on her face as we head for the stairs. "It's killing me, you know. Not having a clue what we're doing."

I give a short laugh. "That was part of the plan, babe."

"To torment me?"

"To help you relax. Loosen up a bit. Let other people take control for a while, so you don't have to."

She pauses at the front of my truck and blinks those copper eyes up at me, as if just realizing what I figured out the first night we met.

"You can let go with me, darlin'. I'm not going to hurt you."

Her brow lifts ever so slightly, but the emotion in her eyes —the hope—is clear. She wants to trust me. Maybe already does. And it's not something she's used to feeling.

As angry as it makes me that some asshole would hurt her so badly that she'd close herself off the way she has, a sick and twisted part of me is glad it happened, because I want to be the guy she takes a chance on again. The one she opens up to and lets in where every other guy has failed.

ALANA

"Okay, you can come out now." Holden opens the passenger door with a wide grin. He's dressed in my favorite black T-shirt and a backward ball cap, and he's apparently decided to try out a beard, because his stubble is thicker than normal and trimmed up nice and neat, as well.

"I like what you're doing here." I reach out and run my fingers along the light brown hair before letting them glide down his neck and to his chest. "I like all of it actually. A lot."

A low laugh rumbles in his throat before he reaches in and physically lifts me from the seat. "You keep touching me like that and this date is gonna take an obscene turn."

I giggle, loving that he doesn't put me down right away. Instead, he leans in and kisses me slow and deep until my head begins to spin.

"Wow," I sigh against his lips when we finally break apart, both of us breathing a little heavier. "You've definitely upped your game tonight, cowboy."

He chuckles and carefully lowers me to the grass. "You ain't seen nothing yet, darlin'. Come on."

Taking my hand, he leads me toward the old covered bridge that leads people in and out of Mason Creek. It's a gorgeous structure, easily the most historic landmark in town and preserved to its original deep red color.

Aiden and I used to ride our bikes into town when we were kids so we could fish off of the bank, and Madelyn and

I loved to climb up beneath the ends of the bridge and hide out when we wanted to get away from our brothers.

Holden leads me toward one of those banks near one of those ends, and I gasp as soon as I see what he's done.

The white twinkling lights are draped around a couple of the bridge's beams, and there's a blanket with a half dozen pillows spread out beneath them. There's also a picnic basket and a bouquet of wildflowers, and the soft, romantic chords of an old Keith Whitley song hang softly in the air.

"Holden…" I stop short, my hand to my chest, as I take it all in. "Where did you… how did you…"

He wraps an arm around my shoulders and presses a kiss to my temple. "Do you like it?"

"I love it," I whisper, trying my best not to cry, because in all of my twenty-five years, no one has ever done anything like this for me.

"I thought you might. Come and sit."

In a matter of minutes, we're both situated on the blanket, a glass of wine in my hand and a bottle of Coors in his. The warm evening breeze carries the fresh, comforting scent of the creek, but Holden's presence and sexy, citrusy aroma are far more intoxicating.

"I can't believe you did this." I turn to him, still in awe.

One corner of his mouth lifts in a smirk. "Because you didn't think I was capable?"

I shake my head. "I've already figured out that you're the kind of guy who will always rise to the challenge."

"Damn right I will." He leans back on one hand and takes a pull from his beer. "So, am I to assume you've never been on a picnic here or that no one's ever planned a romantic date for you before?"

Damn, he's good.

"Both are true," I admit with ease he's hugely responsible for. "I'm kind of glad for that right now."

He glances my way, one brow arched. "Yeah?"

"Experiencing both with you is pretty nice."

He gives a slow, pleased smile. "You starting to get sweet on me, darlin'?"

I roll my eyes even as I blush. "Do you have a birthday coming up? I'm buying a leash for that ego of yours."

Laughing, he sits up again and leans in for a kiss. "My birthday is in November, but let's be honest—we both know you like my ego."

"Ugh." I push him away and he only laughs harder.

"Don't get hangry, babe. I brought plenty of food."

And he isn't lying. He brought chicken salad, croissants, three kinds of pasta, a cheese and olive assortment, blondies, and the lightest, creamiest lemon cake I've ever had.

"This is to die for." I close my eyes and moan around my fork.

"It came highly recommended from Joy at The Sweet Spot. She said you weren't a big fan of chocolate."

"You told her it was for me?" A warm wave of those silly butterflies whirls in my stomach again as he nods. "Who's sweet on who, cowboy?"

He chuckles and sets his empty plate to the side. "Unlike you, I have no problem admitting it."

"Unlike me?" I shove at his denim-covered thigh. "You think I'd wear this dress for just anyone?"

His dark, satisfied gaze locks on mine. "Keep talking, darlin'."

"You're also the only one I let use my shower, drink my coffee, lounge on my couch, and sleep in my bed."

He dips his chin. "That's what I like to hear."

"You're ridiculous."

"And you're mine."

My mouth falls open in a silent gasp.

"I know we started this thing to show the other guys in

town that you're on the market again, but I'm not a fan of that idea anymore."

"Oh." I'm not sure I was ever a fan, but that's beside the point. Is he saying what I think he's saying?

"I don't know what's going to happen with my other job or where I'm even going to be in a few weeks, but I do know that I want us to keep seeing each other. Some way, somehow."

My heart rises like it's being carried off by those darn butterflies that have taken up residence inside of me. "I-I think I'd like that."

Relief washes over his handsome face and he reaches up and strokes his thumb along my jaw. "I know it's only been a short time, but I can't help but feel like maybe us meeting like this was supposed to happen."

I nod, because I've thought the same. I just tried not to give it much attention in case he didn't feel the same.

"I really like you," I whisper, lifting shaky fingers to his chest. "But I'm also terrified. My past experience—"

"I'm not going to hurt you, Alana," he says softly, leaning in to press his lips to mine. "At least not if I can help it."

And I believe him.

I believe this man that came out of nowhere and turned my life upside down. Or maybe he turned it upside right. I don't know and it doesn't matter, because what I do know is that nothing has felt as right in a very long time.

We pack up the food and lie back on the blanket and the pillows, talking about everything and nothing until the stars come out and the occasional traffic passing over the bridge goes quiet.

"Holden?" I ask, the one subject we haven't touched on refusing to be ignored in the back of my mind.

"Yeah, babe?" With his arm wrapped around my shoulders, he kisses the top of my head.

"Aiden wanted you to tell me something and I told you it didn't matter. I want you to know that it truly doesn't. Not to me anyway. But if it's something you want me to know or something you need to talk about, I'm here."

He goes still beside me and I hold my breath. We've kept our relationship light until now, but if we're going to see how far we can take this, we need to be open with each other, too. More, I want him to know that he doesn't need to hold back with me. Ever.

I turn to face him, my cheek resting on his bicep as our eyes meet. "I want to know everything about you," I say softly. "If we're going to keep seeing each other—"

"I'm a bull rider," he confesses and my exhale feels like it goes on forever.

"I know," I admit, too. "Or rather, I guessed."

"Really?"

I nod. "It's the only thing I could think of that Aiden would be so insistent I know."

"Your ex, huh?"

"Yeah."

His fingers glide behind my ear with a strand of hair and I sigh. "Do you want to talk about it?"

"No. It was a long time ago and he doesn't matter anymore. But you…" I press my palm to his chest, feeling his heart beat beneath it. "You do matter. So if you want to tell me, I'm happy to listen."

His eyes dart back and forth between mine for a long beat before he pulls in a breath and exhales the truth, "I'm pro and the boss I mentioned is the ABR."

Shit. I mean, the possibility had crossed my mind, but to hear him confirm it…

"I was accused of the assault after a ride in Tulsa and cleared just like I told you. Instead of supporting me, the ABR decided I needed a hiatus. They said it was to protect me from the media and to let the story die off, but it couldn't be any more obvious that they're only trying to protect themselves."

"That's awful, Holden. I'm so sorry."

He swallows. "Me, too. I'm sorry I gave so much of myself to them. That I put my body through so much shit just to give them a show. Don't get me wrong—I've wanted to ride pro since I was a kid—but it wasn't just the titles I was after. I wanted to be part of something bigger than myself. The rodeo family. The brotherhood…"

His face contorts with a flash of emotion that's gone just as quickly as it came, and my heart aches for him. Our situations are different but similar. I know how it feels to work so hard and think your life is headed in one direction, only to have someone else yank the reins and stop it all.

"I'm not sure I even want to go back anymore," he says quietly. The sadness in his voice is as clear as the moon rising in the sky, but so is the conviction. "If anyone is going to decide my future, it's going to be me."

"What will you do if you don't go back?" I ask, stroking his eyebrow with my thumb.

"Would you think I was crazy if I said I wanted to do some more ranching?"

"At Wilder's?" My silly heart swells at the thought of him sticking around, but I tamp it down, not wanting to get my hopes up.

"Not sure. I'd like to have my own place someday, but that's a hell of an undertaking."

"I know a little something about that." I smile and bop his nose with my fingertip. He reaches up and snags my hand.

"What I do for a living doesn't freak you out?" he asks, his lips lingering against the pulse in my wrist.

"It probably should, but it doesn't." I should be concerned about how well he knows Cory, because he undoubtedly does. In fact, I'd be an idiot not to realize the connection between Holden and Aiden—and now Mason Creek—is none other than my bull rider ex-boyfriend.

But I don't want to know, because I don't want it to matter. I don't want it to change anything between us.

"I'm so fucking glad to hear that." His hand slides around the back of my neck, tugging me close for a kiss. A kiss that's intentional and precise, all firm lips and coaxing tongue that makes me forget that we're outside, lying on the bank of the creek, until a vehicle passes over the bridge.

"Oh my god," I half groan, half laugh. "They can probably see us down here, making out like teenagers."

Without a word, Holden reaches back, gives a tug, and the twinkle lights go dark. "Problem solved."

I giggle and bury my face in his chest. "They'll still see your truck and know we're here."

"Then we'd better be quick."

Before I can ask what he means, he rolls over and braces himself above me, elbows on either side of my head.

"Of course, we could wait until we get home, but what's the fun in that?" He waggles his eyebrows and then his mouth is on my jaw and my neck and my collarbone. Goose bumps rise on my skin as Kane Brown starts to sing "Like a Rodeo" on Holden's phone.

"We can't do this right here," I say, though my protest is more of a breathless moan than an objection. The arch of my back when his hot, wet tongue sweeps across the swell of my cleavage is even more pathetic.

He chuckles, and in seconds, both of my breasts are freed to the night and his eager mouth. When his lips close around one nipple and then the other, I couldn't argue if I wanted to.

"Love these so fucking much," he murmurs, before he dives back in again, sucking and teasing me until I'm a mess of lust and longing beneath him.

"I want to touch you," I rasp, shoving a hand between us so I can palm his erection through his jeans. But it isn't enough. I need to feel his silky skin against mine, so I work his fly free until I can wrap my hand around him.

He groans and his hips twitch, his cock thrusting into my eager grip. "Thought we couldn't do this," he grits out, his jaw clenched.

"We shouldn't." But that doesn't mean we can't. "Flip over."

His brow creases, but when I shove at his chest, he gives in.

"*Fuuuck*." His hips flex to meet mine when I straddle his lap and rub myself, still covered in panties, over his length. "You're soaked," he grunts, his big hands curling around my hips to keep our contact and the friction tight. "Just a shift of that fabric and I could be buried inside you."

"And no one would see a thing," I pant, already lifting just enough to do exactly that.

He reaches between us, as well, holding himself steady as I sink down on his length until I can't take anymore.

It feels like heaven, being full of him like this. The heat from his body radiating into mine, the slow, sensual slide of skin on skin, the way his eyes lock on mine as I move…

"Feels so fucking good," he grunts, our bodies rocking in unison, chasing that inevitable high together. "Never expected to find this. Never expected to find *you*…"

All I can do is nod, because the emotion is building as quickly in my chest as my orgasm is low in my belly. "I'm going to come," I whimper, and with two strokes of Holden's thumb over my clit, I'm there, biting back my cry as my body clenches around his.

"That's it, baby, take what you need," he praises, his hips bucking harder and faster until his head snaps back and he lets go, too.

For several long moments, we do nothing but lie on the blanket beneath the moonlight, catching our breaths while the frogs and crickets chatter.

And then he presses a kiss to my forehead and repeats his words from earlier—*you're mine*—and I know it's true.

This man already owns more than my body... he owns my heart, too.

CHAPTER 17

HOLDEN

The next week flies by in a blur. Between busting my ass at the Roman Wilde Ranch and spending my evenings loving on Alana, I haven't had a spare minute to myself. Don't get me wrong—I'm not complaining. Keeping busy has kept my mind off the ABR, but it's also kept me from sitting down and taking a deeper look at my finances.

Wilder drove over to Magnolia Blue midweek to meet with Sandy and Grady Jackson from DreamBig Real Estate. He said things went well, but Grady had to gather some more information before he could give Sandy a confident appraisal.

Obviously, I know these things take time, but I'm chomping at the bit. I want to know exactly what I'm looking at before I let myself get too excited about it. And I want to be prepared to move fast when the numbers do come in, because if I can afford the Magnolia Blue, then I need to make Sandy an offer before someone else does.

So, that's why I'm sitting alone in the stable on Friday, keeping out of the sun while I mull over my thoughts and nosh on a sandwich. My phone vibrates in my pocket and I smile. Probably Alana wanting to confirm our plans for drinks and dancing at Pony Up tonight. Only it's not her name on the screen—it's Cory's.

Cory, who hasn't so much as texted or called once since I've been in Mason Creek, despite connecting me with the place.

"If you're trying to sell me something, it better be beer," I say by way of greeting.

Cory snorts. "I'm more likely to peddle whiskey, but if you need beer, I can hook you up."

I make a throaty sound at the same time Diego, Levi's pride and joy Palomino, whinnies in the stall behind me.

"You out at Wilder's?"

"As if I'd be anywhere else." Other than Alana's, that is. Which I'd tell him about if I wasn't so irritated with his ghost act these past few weeks.

"Don't get salty with me. I'm the one who got you the gig, remember?" He laughs and I roll my head from side to side, trying to snap the tension.

Yeah, he got me here, and he was right about Mason Creek taking my mind off the ABR. But he was supposed to be my insider, too. He was supposed to find out what the hell was going on, so I'd have ammunition with CJ. Apparently he forgot about that part of our conversation.

"How's the circuit?" I sneer, the sarcasm in my tone is thicker than I intended, but fuck it. I don't give a shit if I sound bitter, because I fucking am bitter.

"Same old, same old. Took second in Vegas last weekend. Friggin' Marciano drew Atlas, so of course, he came out on top. Lucky fucker always gets the easy bulls."

I grunt. Lucas Marciano is one hell of a rider, but he's also one of the cockiest pricks in the ABR. He and Cory have gone back and forth in points all season, and as much as I'd like to see Marciano taken down a notch, I don't know if Cory has it in him this year.

"Have you heard anything from CJ about coming back?" my buddy asks.

"Not since he called to tell me there'd been another assault."

Cory sighs. "Yeah. I heard Vickie got roughed up. I haven't seen her, but Heidi said she went home to California. You probably knew that, though."

I frown. "Why would I know that?"

"You and Vickie. You've got that thing going…"

"Bro, I know you've been busy screwing around with Heidi, but you need to pay more attention. Vickie and I haven't so much as carried on as much as a two-minute conversation since last fall."

"You don't need to talk to fuck, man."

He's lucky he's not standing in front of me right now or I'd punch him in the face, solely on account of being such a dumbass.

"Anyway…" he continues on. "Things have been quiet. I was hoping that meant CJ would give you the green light."

I shake my head, almost as resigned as I am irritated. "Nope. Haven't heard a word and I'm not sure I'd jump if he called anyway."

"What do you mean?" Cory asks.

"I mean I'm pissed. This whole situation is bullshit and I'm done taking it up the ass for no good reason. I'm about ready to tell the ABR to—"

"Don't, dude. Don't let this get to your head and make you say or do something you'll regret. How many times have we talked about rising to the top together?"

I grimace. Yeah, we had plans to kick ass and take names and for the most part, we've done it. But do I really give a shit about being on top of an organization that doesn't give a shit about me?

"I don't know, man." I take off my Stetson and push a hand through my hair. "I don't know what the hell I'm gonna do."

"Just keep doing what you're doing in Mason Creek. The press is dying down and this will get sorted out before you know it."

Maybe, maybe not. And do I even care?

"Listen, I called because I'm hoping you'll ride with me in the rodeo Labor Day weekend. Since you're there and all."

"You're coming to Mason Creek?"

"Yeah. It's been a while and my mom's been on my ass about it. I also have some personal shit to take care of, so I figured why not?"

I nod. "Yeah, I've heard your mom raising hell on the other end of the phone before."

He laughs.

"But I'm not sure me riding is a good idea. I'm here to lie low and not draw attention, remember?"

"Eh. The rodeo is still a week away and a lot could happen in seven days. Who knows? Maybe CJ will call."

Yeah, well, CJ can blow me.

"I've already told the committee I'm coming and that I might bring a friend. The spot is yours if you want it."

I'm not going to lie—the thought of riding again has my hands flexing and my heart racing. I haven't touched a rope in weeks and the prospect of hearing that horn sound and seeing that gate open is tempting.

And even though Alana isn't a fan of bull riding, part of me wants to show her what I can do. Even if I walk away from the pro circuit, I'm always going to be a bull rider and I want to show her that not all of us are assholes. She'd just ridden the wrong cowboy.

"I'll think about it," I finally say, though the idea grows more appealing by the second. If I'm going to leave the ABR, why the hell should I keep hiding?

"You do that. In the meantime, don't do anything stupid."

"Not making any promises."

He starts to say something else, but Wilder strolls into the stable, pointing at his watch.

"Sorry, man, but I gotta go." I don't bother waiting for a goodbye before I disconnect the call and get back to work.

ALANA

"Cleanup needed in aisle four," Susie says when I emerge from my office just after noon. My head is throbbing from crunching numbers all morning and I'm in desperate need of a break and a gigantic cup of coffee.

"Where's Pete?" I glance toward the cash registers through aching, squinted eyes.

"Helping Nancy move things around in the deli cooler."

"Well, he can stop doing that for a few minutes and get the mess cleaned up. What is it anyway?"

"Coconut oil. Granny Char dropped not one, but two of the bulk-sized jars."

Jesus. I don't even want to think about why the dirty old lady is buying coconut oil. "Well, tell Pete to use some Dawn on the floor, too. We don't need that tile getting slick."

Susie's eyes widen and I know she's wondering why I'm not rushing to aisle four to do the cleanup myself like I normally would.

"My brain hurts from all of the math I just did," I explain. "And I need to run to the bank."

She nods. "Go and get some air."

"I think I will. Hold down the fort while I'm gone."

"You got it, boss." Susie touches two fingers to her forehead and I give a silent laugh. An actual one would hurt too much.

Fifteen minutes later, with the banking complete, I head across the town square and straight to Java Jitters like my life depends on it.

"I'll take the biggest, strongest cup of coffee you have," I tell Jessie as greeting.

My friend and also the owner of the quaint little shop smiles sympathetically. "Bad day, huh?"

"I was mathing," I explain, and she gives a resolute nod.

"Say no more." She goes to work behind the counter and hands over a huge iced coffee a minute later. "It's too hot for a regular cup and I know you like the iced stuff better anyway."

"I love you." My lips connect with the straw and I moan as the cool liquid hits my tongue.

Jessie laughs. "Do you need a moment? Maybe someplace private?"

I take another long drink and sigh. "Nah, I'm good now. But this *is* orgasmic."

"Like the one you had down by the creek last Friday night?"

My shoulders snap back at the familiar voice behind me.

"Don't worry, honey. No one but Hazel and I saw."

My face bursts into flames and it takes everything I have in me to turn to Hattie Jackson and not crumble into a pile of ash at her feet.

Her knowing smile stretches a little wider when our eyes meet and I know. I just know she saw it all.

"I'm so happy for you." The older woman reaches out and pats my arm. "He seems like such a nice young man. And he's built well, too, if you know what I mean."

*Dear God, if you're listening, please take me now. Right here in the middle of the coffee shop. I'm ready to go.*

"For what it's worth, Hazel and I debated long and hard—no pun intended—about whether or not we should tell Tate. And we almost decided that your privacy was more important. Until we realized that *you* clearly didn't care about privacy when you decided to mount your stallion right there for anyone to see."

Shit. Shit, shit, shit. I clench my eyes shut and rub at my forehead. "When did you tell her?"

"Just this morning."

Which means the story could go live any minute now. Great. Just freaking great.

"It's nothing to be embarrassed about, honey. In fact, I'm pretty sure everyone in town is going to be over the moon, knowing you're finally over that Mitchell boy. We just want you to be happy, sweetheart."

Uh huh, sure. Also, I am certain that not everyone is going to be as thrilled as she thinks they'll be. Namely my father and Aiden.

"Anyway, I just wanted you to know." Hattie gives my arm a gentle squeeze and turns on the heels of her Mary Jane's before heading out of the coffee shop like her sole purpose was to follow me inside and drop her bomb.

"If it's any consolation, Tate already posted today," Jessie speaks up behind me. "So, you're probably safe until tomorrow."

Well, at least there's that.

*THE JACKSON SISTERS **caught us at the creek last week. They saw it all**,* I text Holden when I get back to the market. He mentioned something about starting an addition on one of the barns today, so I'm not surprised that it takes him a couple of hours to reply.

*Hot damn. Well, I hope they'd enjoyed the show.*

*Holden Daniel! They saw us having sex!*

*Darlin', we were dressed. They couldn't have seen much.*

I groan, practically hearing the amusement in his words.

*According to Hattie, you're a stallion, so I wouldn't be so sure about that.*

My phone rings a second later.

"She said I was hung?" Holden laughs as soon as I click onto the call. "I mean, I can think of worse rumors to be spread."

"Oh my god, stop." I can't help but laugh, too. "My brother is going to hear about this. And my dad."

"Eh. Your dad likes me."

"Only for twenty more hours until Tate tells all of Mason Creek just how neighborly I've been."

He snorts. "You did put together one hell of a welcome package, I'll give you that."

"Holden!"

"Sorry!" Only, he starts laughing all over again, completely contradicting himself. "Babe, it's going to be fine."

Uh huh. At least the shock made my heart beat so fast that my headache went away in record time.

"We're still on for tonight, right? I can't wait to twirl you around the dance floor."

I pinch the bridge of my nose and sigh. "Yes, we're still on. In fact, we should make the most of tonight, because I'm going into hiding as soon as Tate's story goes live."

"That doesn't sound like such a horrible situation, either. The two of us holed up together for a few days…"

I roll my eyes at his playful insinuation. "I have to get back to work."

"Yep, me too. Can't wait to show you off tonight, darlin.'"

## CHAPTER 18

HOLDEN

"*P*eople are looking at us funny."

"No, they aren't, babe. But if they are, it's only because you look fucking hot." I bury my face in Alana's neck and inhale. Not only is she rocking a pair of tight jeans and an equally snug red tank top, she smells like absolute heaven. "You're making my mouth water. If we weren't already in trouble, I'd drag you into a back room and devour you."

She shivers and I feel her nipples pebble against my chest. "You're going to get me run out of town, Colorado."

"That's all right, baby, you can just come back home with me."

She laughs, but I'm not kidding. I want this girl with me wherever I go.

"Jesus, you two," Wilder chastises above the music. Once again, Tucker Simms is on stage, singing eighties and nineties country songs to Pony Up's wall-to-wall crowd. "If you're going to grope each other, at least do it on the dance floor so it's less obvious."

"No, no, Wilder James." Alana shakes a cherry red-polished fingertip at our friend. "You don't get to give us a hard time about this, because if you and Aiden hadn't invited him here, this would have never happened."

A slightly drunken Hallie pops her lips. "She's right, babe. This really is your fault."

Wilder scoffs. "Actually, if we're placing blame, I'm pretty sure Cory—"

"Oh! It's my favorite song!" Alana throws her arms in the air, as Tucker starts crooning Keith Whitley's "Don't Close Your Eyes." "We gotta dance again, cowboy. Come on."

Wilder and I exchange 'what the hell did we get ourselves into' glances, before I set my beer on the table and let her tug me onto the dance floor for the tenth time tonight.

She loops her arms around my neck and crushes her soft body to mine as we fall into rhythm with the song, swaying back and forth like we're the only two people in the bar.

"Remember the first time we danced here?" she asks, her fingers sliding into my hair. "I wanted to hate you so badly, but then you made me dance with you and I was a goner."

I chuckle into her ear. "My moves were that good, huh?"

"Actually, it was because you'd saved me from falling on my ass, and then when we danced, you held me like I was something precious. Something you needed to protect."

"You are precious, babe. But you're tough as nails, too."

She smiles up at me softly. "Yes, but I love that I don't have to be with you. I can let down my walls, knowing you'll keep me safe."

Her words hit me like a hoof to the chest and for a moment it's hard to breathe. This girl has come to mean so fucking much to me and there isn't a thing I wouldn't do for her.

I reach up to tuck her hair behind her ear and trail my

knuckles down the side of her face. "I'll always protect you, darlin'. That's my job."

"Your job?"

"Not only as your current boyfriend, but as the guy who's hoping to be your last."

Her eyes go wide. "Holden…"

"I know it's soon, but it's how I feel. You're the one I—"

She toes up and presses her lips to mine before I can finish the declaration. "You're the one I want, too, cowboy."

*Hell yes.* My arms tighten around her and I'm not sure how long we stand there kissing like no one's watching, but eventually it registers that Tucker isn't even singing anymore. An upbeat pop song thumps through the bar's sound system instead.

"Now people are definitely looking at us," Alana sighs, hiding her face in my T-shirt.

A quick glance around the packed bar confirms it. "Yep, they are."

"Oh my god." She laughs and quickly tugs me back to our table, where Wilder smirks behind the lip of his beer.

"Y'all really need to knock this shit off. Starting to feel like *Roadhouse* in here."

I give him a smug grin and reach for my own beer when none other than Cory Mitchell materializes from the crowd.

"What the hell, man? You didn't tell me you were coming —" The words die on my tongue when I realize his focus isn't on me, but on Alana.

Alana, who's gone stock still. Possibly not even breathing. Instinctively, my arm slides around her waist to make sure she's okay, and Cory gives a bark of laughter.

"Really, McMurray? This is how you've been spending your time?" He shakes his head, and even in the shadow of his white Stetson, I can see the contempt in his eyes.

And that's when it hits me. Holy shit.

He's the cheating asshole bull rider ex.

How *the fuck* did I miss that?

"You come to my hometown and you hook up with my girl?" He takes a predatory step forward, his nostrils flaring as he shifts his heated gaze between me and Alana.

"I'm most definitely not your girl, Cory. So quit the caveman act." She turns toward the table, rolling her eyes, and his jaw tightens as he glares down at her.

"I thought you quit bull riders, baby girl. Or were you just waiting for my replacement to come along?"

I surge around her so quickly, putting myself between them, that she gasps, even as Cory gives a sardonic laugh.

"Holden, don't!" She tries to push between us, but Wilder intervenes first, corralling Cory back toward the exit.

"Nope, we're not doing this here," he warns. "Outside before Emma calls her fiancé and someone ends up in jail."

Cory snorts. "Shit, I'd love to see Aiden right now. Does he know you're doing his baby sister, Mack? Don't fucking tell me she's the reason you're quitting the ABR."

The bar's screen door slams shut behind us and Wilder gives Cory a pointed shove. "Mitchell, so help me God, I'll beat your ass myself if you disrespect her again."

"Disrespect her?" Cory roars. "What about this son of a bitch disrespecting *me*? I'm the one who told him to come here. I'm the one who got him a goddamn job when his little fuckup cost him his spot on the trail."

"Are you friggin' serious?" I laugh, but there's no humor in it. "You know damn well I didn't do anything wrong."

"Do I?" Cory sneers. "Because if memory serves me correctly, this isn't the first time a girl has come forward where you're concerned."

My blood runs cold and it's all I can do not to pummel his smug face. "What in the hell are you talking about?"

He shakes his head in disgust and I can't tell if he actually believes the bullshit he just insinuated or if he's that good of an actor. "And to think you fell for this asshole," he says, swinging his bitter gaze to Alana.

Fuck. Alana.

I turn to see her trembling a few feet away. Closer to me than him, but still out of reach. "Baby, he's talking out of his ass. I've never—"

"Stop," she pleads. "Just stop. Both of you."

"Alana, you don't even know this guy. He—"

"I said stop!" Her quiet plea turns to rage as she spins toward Cory with her hands fisted against her thighs. "You don't get to come back after four goddamn years and pretend you give a shit!"

Cory's face pales. "Alana, I've always cared. You know I have. I even told Aiden…"

"No, Cory," she snaps. "Just… no."

Hope flares in my chest, because she has to believe me, right?

But then she turns and the sudden sadness in her eyes is like a knife to my gut.

"I can't do this." Her voice cracks and I see the shine of tears in her eyes. "I'm sorry."

"Baby, come on…" I reach for her, needing to touch her and reassure her. Something. But she takes two steps back and my hand falls just like my heart.

Ten minutes ago, she told me she wanted me.

And now she's walking away.

ALANA

"I'm here and I have alcohol." Emma busts through the

door of Hawkins' Bed & Breakfast's honeymoon suite, her arms full of booze and Solo cups.

I give an exhausted laugh from the corner of the loveseat where I've been curled up since Hallie ushered me inside an hour ago. I'm not sure how she did it, but by the time we walked from Pony Up to my apartment, the room was booked and Levi was waiting to give us a ride.

"Aren't you supposed to be working?" I ask as she unloads the bottles she clearly swiped from the bar and begins pouring.

"Jack offered to close up." She hands me a cup with a hefty shot of whiskey and my stomach turns.

"I'm not drinking this." I shove it back at her. "I'd hate myself in the morning and I don't get wasted over Cory Mitchell anymore, remember?"

"Fuck Cory," Hallie scoffs from the bed. "I don't even know the guy and I disliked him the second I saw him."

"Mmm hmm." Emma purses her lips and takes a seat on the edge of the bed. "But I don't think he's the guy we're avoiding right now."

*Ugh.* Closing my eyes, I let my head fall back against the sofa and Holden's face is right there, his panic as clear as the stars in the sky when I turned and left him in the Pony Up parking lot.

I'd suspected he knew Cory. Even guessed that Cory was the one who'd connected him to Aiden and Wilder. But I didn't expect the reality check that had slapped me across the face when I saw them in the same room together.

"Did you know?" Emma asks, her brow furrowed. "That he was really a bull rider and not just a ranch hand?"

I nod and hug my knees a little tighter to my chest. "He told me. About the ABR and the assault accusation, too."

"Do you think…" Hallie hesitates. "Do you think there's any truth to what Cory said about another girl?"

"Not even a little." It was a load of BS intended solely to make me question Holden's character. Typical Cory behavior.

"Then why are we here, exactly?" Emma asks, her frown deepening.

"Because I was stupid," I admit, emotion building fast in my chest all over again. "Because after four years of telling myself I'd never be weak for a man again, I had to go and fall for the one guy I've always known couldn't stay."

"Oh, sweetie…" Hallie hops off the bed and comes to sit next to me on the loveseat. "He said that? That he's leaving?"

"He's said it from the start. He's only in Mason Creek until the assault story disappears and the ABR lets him ride again."

"What about a long distance relationship? It's obvious you two have something special."

I shake my head and swipe at my tears. "I tried that with Cory and it was too much. Him being on the road all the time and mismatched schedules… I'd almost forgotten about all of that until I saw him tonight."

"It's not my business, but Wilder said something about Holden quitting the rodeo. Cory brought it up, too. Do you think—"

"I won't let him quit."

Emma's brows dart up. "It's kind of not up to you."

"I know that. But he's not quitting for the right reasons. He's doing it because of other people's shitty decisions. And we all know that's a disaster in the making."

Hallie places her hand on my arm. "Maybe he's outgrown it. Maybe—"

"People don't outgrow things they're passionate about."

Seeing Cory again reminded me of that. I'd always known he had rodeo dreams. I'd grown up watching him and Aiden and Wilder at the ranch, and in high school, Mads and I had followed them around from rodeo to rodeo. Riding had been a good time for my brother and Wilder, but to Cory, it was the beginning of something bigger.

Something I could never measure up to, no matter how hard I tried.

I'm not so arrogant to think that a man I've known for a matter of weeks would give up his career for me, but Cory's words tonight... they hit a nerve.

And they made me realize that I can't let Holden walk away. I can't let him give up on something he loves, certainly not because he was made to feel like he didn't matter.

"He matters to me," I rasp, pressing my fingers to my chest. "And if I have to prove that by helping yet another cowboy realize that his real passion in life is something other than me, then that's what I have to do."

## CHAPTER 19

HOLDEN

*T*he buzz of my phone breaks into the sleep I'd only found a couple of hours earlier on Wilder's couch. For a solid ten seconds, I ignore it, because there's not a single person I want to talk to right now.

Well, except for Alana.

Shit, what if it's her?

I jolt upright and knock over a bottle of water, trying to reach my cell on the coffee table. And then I almost throw the fucking thing across the room when CJ's name shows on the display.

No way am I talking to him right now. Cory probably called him last night and fed him a bunch of shit just like he did with Alana, and I'm not playing that damn game right now.

I reject the call and scrub my hands over my face only to have the friggin' thing ring again, because that's how CJ is when he's got a wild hair up his ass.

"What?" I snarl, putting the call on speaker.

"Well, good morning to you, too, sunshine."

I pinch the bridge of my nose and seriously consider firing him on the spot just for being so fucking annoying. And then I remember we have a contract.

"What do you want?" I ask again, my words as tight as the tension in my neck and shoulders, a small part of which is the result of crashing on Wilder and Hallie's couch and the rest from worrying myself crazy about Alana.

"You know, I expected you'd be a little more grateful to hear from me."

I open my mouth to tell him to fuck off when his words register. "You're calling to tell me I can come back?"

"Yeah, you cranky fucker. The girl in Tulsa? Turns out she was banging her best friend's boyfriend. Got busted stumbling out of a back room at a bar, so she made up some bullshit story. Blamed it on a bull rider since a bunch of the guys were at the bar that night after the ride. And Vickie? That was a completely unrelated event."

I stare down at my phone as the past few weeks flash before my eyes. Is he friggin' serious right now? I put up with all of this BS because some sorority girl decided to be a shit friend?

"Mack? You there?" CJ asks, and I rub my eyes.

"Yeah, I'm here." I'm not sure how I feel about any of it, but I'm here.

"Dallas has already given you the green light. I told him you probably won't be ready to ride next weekend in California, but you'd be on the ticket for Lincoln the weekend after."

I grunt. "And what if I don't want to?"

"Don't want to wait? I mean, I guess that's up to you."

"I mean what if I don't want to ride? What if I don't want to come back?"

He's silent for a long moment before he laughs. "Yeah, right."

His reaction makes my lip curl. Does he honestly expect me to come back like none of this happened? Like the ABR didn't turn their back on me and treat me like a damn pariah?

"What's Dallas gonna do to make this right by me?" The ABR CEO and master puppeteer never even bothered to talk to me himself about this shit, so I'm not holding my breath that he'll care much now.

CJ sighs. "Nothing, man. It's not his fault any more than it's yours."

I give a bitter laugh. "Yet I was punished for it. Fuck that. Fuck him."

"He did what he could, Mack. He was in a tough spot, too."

I shake my head. "You know, I've had a lot of time to think these past few weeks and I'm not sure that's good enough."

"I know it sucks, but you have to understand…"

"Actually, I don't. The ABR showed their true colors and I'm not a fan. I may love riding, but I like my integrity more. I'm not about to turn a cheek and pretend this never happened. As far as I'm concerned, the ABR can kiss my ass."

"You don't mean that." CJ laughs. Honest to God fucking laughs, like this whole thing is nothing more than a joke to him. "Just get your ass back to Colorado by Monday."

"Don't hold your breath." I end the call and give the phone a toss across the table.

"Sounds like you could use some coffee," Wilder's sleep-roughened voice comes from the kitchen and I fall against the back of the couch with a frustrated huff.

"I could use some actual sleep, but it's too friggin' late for that." It's going on eight o'clock and I'm not going to waste any more time waiting on Alana to answer my texts or calls. As soon as I'm caffeinated, I'm finding her and we're having this out.

"She respond yet?" Wilder asks as if reading my mind while he messes around with the coffee pot.

"Nope." And all of my texts are unread, too.

"Hallie took her to Emma's bed-and-breakfast last night."

Right. Because if she went home, she might run into me, which she's obviously trying to avoid. Fucking Cory.

"Where's Mitchell stay when he's in Mason Creek?" I ask, knowing damn well Wilder isn't going to tell me.

He laughs. "Nice try, man."

"What?" I chuckle, too, because if I don't, I might very well cry. How could Cory say that shit? I mean, yeah, finding out he's Alana's ex was just as much of a surprise for me as seeing us together must have been for him.

But they've been done for four years now, right?

*I have some personal shit to take care of.*

*I've always cared. You know I have. I even told Aiden.*

His words replay in my head and I curse under my breath.

How the hell was I supposed to know he still had a thing for her? In the four years we've been on the trail together, he never once mentioned her. Never even hinted at having a girl back home he still cared about.

Knowing wouldn't have changed anything. Or maybe that's what I want to believe, because I don't want it to matter. I took one look at that girl and I knew. I fucking knew she was something special.

I love her sass and determination. How she stands her ground and works her ass off, too. But what I love most is how she goes all in with everything she does. Including me.

"Coffee will be done shortly. I'm going to hop in the

shower. Don't do anything stupid." *Like Google the Mitchell's address and go beat Cory's ass* goes unsaid.

"I'll try," I mutter, grabbing my phone from the table to double-check that, nope, Alana still isn't talking to me.

I push to my feet and stalk to the bank of windows in the living room that overlook a wide pasture and the mountains in the distance.

A truck turns into the driveway and dread sinks in my gut.

Aiden.

And he's in his personal vehicle, too, so there's nothing stopping him from giving me a piece of his mind *and* his fist.

I meet him on the porch before he can knock, because there's no point in pretending I don't know exactly why he's here.

He lifts his chin and tightens his jaw when he spots me waiting for him. "McMurray." His tone is as tense as his posture.

"Faulkner." I dip my chin. "If you're here to tell me to stay away from your sister, you should know she's doing a fine job of making that happen herself."

"Good." Then he gestures to the Adirondack chairs. "Sit."

I'm far too old for these kinds of lectures, but I know when to pick my battles, so I sit and eventually he does the same.

Elbows on his knees and hands folded between them, he's quiet for several moments before he speaks. "Cory Mitchell's a fucking tool."

I laugh, instant relief lightening the load on my shoulders. "That is not what I expected you to say."

"Don't think I'm not pissed at you, too, but the shit he tried to pull last night was completely out of line. He started asking about Alana a few months ago and I told him flat out she wasn't interested in going down that road again. Not after the hell he put her through."

"I had no idea," I say, turning to him and shaking my head. "In hindsight, I think you and Wilder were trying to tell me, but it didn't click. And even when she told me her ex was a bull rider, it never crossed my mind that she was talking about him."

"Would it have mattered?"

"I want to say no, but Cory's one of my closest friends. In the ABR and out. We practically live together on the road. That's not something I'd willingly make awkward, you know?"

"Does it matter now that you know?"

I shake my head before he finishes the question. "Not at all. This is about me and her now, no one else."

I expect him to give me an attitude, to tell me I'm not good enough for her or whatever big brothers usually threaten their little sisters' love interests with. But he simply nods and glances out over the field.

"Don't give up on her," he says quietly. "He broke her heart and she spent the last four years building walls around herself to keep it from happening again. For some reason, she let you in. I don't know why now or why you, but I can tell you this—she's been more herself these past few weeks than she's been in years."

And somehow, despite being accused of a heinous crime, having my career nearly ripped from my hands, and being cast away to the middle of nowhere, I've been the happiest I've been in a long time, too.

It's not hard to figure out why. I've had her to come home to. Her to banter with. Her to finally make me acknowledge what I've known for a while now…

Bull riding was meant to be a phase in my life, but not my *entire* life.

"I appreciate that, man." And I mean it. I don't need his permission where Alana is concerned, but knowing I have his respect… it means something. "And I don't plan on letting what happened last night change anything. I just need her to talk to me, so I can explain a few things."

He nods. "I saw her walking in town when I came through."

I jump to my feet. "Headed home?"

"No, but I have a pretty good idea where she was going."

"Okay…" I roll my hand impatiently and he gestures to my feet.

"Get your boots on. You're gonna need 'em."

―――――

I FIND her sitting at the top of a pretty bridge in the middle of the woods with her bare legs and Converse sneakers dangling above the creek.

The only sounds are of water trickling over the rocks in the creek bed and the rustle of leaves in the canopy of trees overhead. Alana had to have heard my truck, but she continues staring out over the creek, unfazed.

"Mind if I join you?" I ask, tucking my sweaty palms into my pockets as I approach, careful not to scare her.

"Of course not." She flicks a quick smile my way and then pats the wood next to her. "Sit on this side. There's a wad of gum on the other."

"Ah, thanks for the heads-up." I chuckle and settle down beside her, sticking my boots and legs between the wrought iron bars, too. "This is an awfully fancy bridge for the middle of the woods, no?"

"Mmm hmm, but there's a really romantic story that accompanies it." She gives me another timid glance, the faintest pink in her cheeks. I don't know what it means, but she didn't tell me to fuck off, so I'll take it.

"Well, you have to tell me now that you mentioned it." I bump my shoulder into hers and she gives a small laugh before tucking a strand of dark hair behind her ear.

"Well, legend has it that, before Mason Creek became the happening little town that it is, a young man named Henry Davis was madly in love with a girl who used to spend her days exploring these woods. But she hated that she could never get to the other side of the creek. So, in the grandest of grand gestures, Henry secretly built the bridge for her. Rumor has it he proposed to her here, too. Obviously she said yes, because hello, he built her a bridge."

I try to bite back a laugh, but fail. "Obviously."

"Hey." She pokes my thigh. "It's sweet and you know it."

"I'm just wondering how he got all of this steel into the woods without her noticing. Especially if she liked coming out here so much."

Her eyebrows dart up. "Are you questioning local legend, Colorado?"

I lift my hands, unable to keep the grin from spreading across my face, *because hello, she's talking to me*. "I'm just saying."

She rolls her eyes, but the twitch of her lips gives her away. And I am so fucking relieved.

"You're so damn cute when you pretend to be annoyed with me."

"I *am* annoyed with you." She huffs and shifts her gaze back to the water. Then, she promptly sighs and shoves a hand through her hair. "Actually, that's not true. It's just... what in the hell was that with Cory?"

I wish I knew. I wish I had something better to say other than, "I'm sorry. I should've figured out he was your ex."

She shakes her head. "I should have told you. I mean, once

you told me about the ABR, I realized he was probably the one who suggested you come to Mason Creek. I should have said something then."

So she had known. I'd wondered when she'd only seemed surprised to see him, not about the things he'd said.

"Nah, babe. I get why you didn't. It was a long time ago. In the past."

She bites her lips together. "Except, the reason I didn't tell you was because I didn't want it to change things with us, not because my past with him is inconsequential. He's obviously a good friend if he connected you with Wilder. Assuming that part of what he said was true, anyway."

"It is." And thank god she realized that most of the other shit he'd said wasn't. "But my friendship with him has nothing to do with me and you."

"Doesn't it?" she counters, her tone almost exasperated as the look in her eyes. "Doesn't it have everything to do with us?"

"You and I are our own thing, babe."

She shakes her head, her eyes bright with unshed tears. "Can you honestly tell me that you would have gotten involved with me if you would have known Cory and I had been involved?"

"What does that matter? I didn't know, and here we are. Me and you. I want to be with you and nothing is going to change that."

Her brow creases. "But he's your friend."

"And you're my girlfriend."

The tears in her eyes shine beneath the morning sun streaking through the trees. "But your friendship with him may be ruined because of me. As much as he hurt me and as much as I wanted to punch him for all of the things he said about you last night, I don't ever want to be the reason you lose something important to you."

Jesus Christ. Doesn't she know that, because of her, I've gained something even more important?

"Babe, listen to me…" I rub a frustrated hand along my jaw. "You might be right about Cory. I might've done the bro code thing and stayed away, but then I would have hated myself because I would have missed this." I curl a hand around her cheek and press my lips to hers before she can stop me. "I would've missed tasting this sassy mouth of yours. I would have missed knowing this smart, sexy, strong-willed woman I can't stop thinking about. I would have missed finding the person I already can't imagine my life without."

"Holden," she breathes my name and the conflict in her eyes breaks my heart.

She doesn't want to make me choose.

But what she doesn't realize is I chose her the second I laid eyes on her.

ALANA

"Not knowing about Cory gave us the chance to find each other. To find something bigger than either of us expected. It was the perfect secret, babe. And I wouldn't change it for anything."

I wouldn't either. In the few weeks I've known Holden, I've grown to care about him in ways I wasn't sure I'd ever be capable of again.

And that's why I can't stand back and watch him poten-tially lose a friend and give up on his career.

"Are you really quitting the ABR?" I ask and his lack of response is telling. "Holden, you can't just quit."

He runs a hand around the back of his neck. "Babe, we've

talked about this. I don't want to give my time and energy to an organization that could give a shit less about me."

"Holden…" I pull my legs from between the bars and turn to face him. "If you quit, you let them win. Don't you see that?"

"I let them win when I let them push me out. I already came up short on that ride, babe."

"But you can go back and show them they screwed up. You can make them regret turning their back on you."

His dark eyes sparkle as he reaches up and cradles my cheek once again. "Darlin', this isn't about vengeance. This is about me taking the reins and making the best decision for me, regardless of what they say."

"And if they say you can come back… Do you honestly think you'll still feel this way?" Because that's my fear. My fear for him is that he'll quit now while his emotions are high and he'll hate himself for it when the dust settles.

I've been down that road. I quit college and quit myself when things with Cory went to crap. Yes, things worked out in the end, but I spent a lot of time being miserable and wishing I'd done things differently.

I don't want that for him.

"You're too good to quit," I tell him. "You might've taken another title this year."

His eyebrows lift over wide brown eyes. "You looked me up."

Crap. "Technically, Hallie did. And then I stole her phone, because Emma confiscated mine."

"And?"

"You're an amazing rider." My shoulders drop and I sigh, because something tells me this isn't an argument I'm going to win. Not right now anyway. "And you look really good in that rodeo vest."

"Just the vest?"

"I'm intentionally trying not to think about the chaps."

His head falls back with a bark of laughter. "Is that why you're so insistent I go back? Because I look good in my gear?"

"I wouldn't mind seeing you up close and personal like that. But I'm serious, Holden. I'm really worried that you're going to make a decision you'll regre—"

"They called me back."

I gasp. "What? When?"

"This morning. Turns out the accusation was bogus." He tells me about the girl and her friend's boyfriend. About the bar and the bull riders. And there's so much frustration in his eyes.

"I see it," I whisper, stroking my fingers along his jaw and then over his eyebrows. "I see it in your face right now. You already know it'll kill you to walk away."

He closes his eyes and his throat works as he swallows. When he speaks, his voice is low and clear. "I've wanted to be a rodeo cowboy since I was four years old and my dad rode over the summer season." His lashes flutter open again and his heavy gaze locks with mine. "But just like my old man, I also knew I wanted a life that didn't revolve around a rodeo schedule.

"I knew this day would come, darlin'. And I knew the decision to walk away from one dream to chase another would hurt a little. I'm not going to pretend it doesn't."

A tear spills down my cheek and he swipes it away.

"I love that you're worried about me," he says softly. "And I understand your fear."

"I quit college. I quit myself. And these past four years have been the hardest of my life."

"But they've been the most rewarding, haven't they?"

"Yes, but…" I pause to swallow. "I don't want you to wake up someday and wish you'd chosen differently."

"Are we talking about bull riding or something else?" He smooths the hair back from my face. "Because if you think for a second that I'll ever regret coming here and falling for you, you're crazy."

"I'd hate myself," I whisper, and when he kisses me again, the hope I've kept sheltered in my heart begins to glow again like a lightning bug in a jar.

"I hate the things I was accused of," he says. "I hate even more that the rodeo didn't support me. But I could never hate you...

"You gave me your heart, darlin', and that's better than any rodeo title."

CHAPTER 20

ALANA

"We weren't supposed to do that."

Holden jogs back into my bedroom with a smile, a wet washcloth, and a bare ass.

"Hell yes, we were." He cleans me up and nuzzles my neck at the same time. "Though, I still think we should've done it on the bridge. I kinda like getting caught with you. Let's everyone know you're mine."

"Let's everyone know I'm a ho for you, too."

"Again, I see no problem."

Ugh.

Tate's online gossip site had been updated bright and early this morning and I'm not sure I'll ever live it down.

*Sorry, Mason Creek bachelors. If you've been patiently waiting for the pretty market manager to open her heart to love once again, you've already missed the boat. Or should we say bull?*

*Last weekend, Alana Faulkner was spotted consummating her relationship with the mysterious ranch hand from*

*Colorado. Except it turns out Holden McMurray isn't
actually a ranch hand at all—he's a world champion bull
rider.*

*Seems as though Ms. Faulkner's contempt for guys in cowboy
boots and chaps has come to an end...*

*And from what we can tell, this cowboy is definitely more than
an eight second ride.*

"It could have been worse, babe. She could have said I was a shitty lay."

"Oh my god!" I shove him away and throw an arm over my eyes, even as I laugh. "This is not funny! My parents are going to hear about this!"

"You think I'll still be invited to dinner tomorrow?"

"HOLDEN!"

He falls back on a pillow, laughing so hard the bed shakes. "You have enough going on in that pretty head of yours. Let me worry about this."

I peek at him from beneath my arm. "But you're not worried."

"Exactly."

I should have let him sit in the gum on the bridge.

"What time did you say you have to be at work?"

"In an hour. I'm closing tonight, since Susie came in for me this morning."

Holden rolls to face me, trailing his fingers lightly over my stomach. "I'm going to talk to Cory while you do that."

"I figured you might."

"I'm going to tell him that we're together. And that I don't give a shit what he thinks about it."

He's going to be the end of me, this one. Death by perpetually guilty conscience. "And if he decides never to talk to you again?"

"He has to. We bought a travel trailer together."

"And now I feel even worse." I sit up and reach for my robe before sliding out of bed.

"Please don't." He meets me at my dresser and turns me to face him before I can grab clean clothes. With a finger, he lifts my chin and forces my eyes on his. "I'm not sure I want to put any more effort into a friendship with someone who'd act like he did last night. He insinuated that I was a friggin' rapist and that's not something I'm sure I can forget, even if he was just spewing shit out of desperation."

The betrayal in his eyes and in his tone makes my heart ache. "I'm so sorry."

"I'm not." His big hands lift to cup my face and he smiles. "I'm not sorry about anything that led me to you."

Before I can argue, his lips are on mine and everything I wanted to protest fades away.

I adore this man. I want him to be happy and to feel valued and loved and respected.

And if he feels those things when he's with me, then maybe he's right where he's supposed to be, after all.

---

"DID you hear about the drama earlier?" Kelly, the night shift deli clerk, asks later that evening as we begin our closing cleanup. The market is technically open for another hour, but Saturday nights are always quiet after the dinner rush.

"Do I want to know?" I bend for the dustpan and toss the dirt and smooshed grapes into the trash.

"Apparently, Sadie's grandma came in and was talking to Nancy about the fancy dinner she had planned for her and Marty tonight."

I grimace, because the idea of Granny Char and Marty dating is still weird as heck to me. Not that people of all ages don't deserve to be happy and find love, but Marty is my boss and Char... well, she's the horniest old woman in town.

"Hattie and Hazel came in, too, and when Hazel overheard Char bragging about her plans, she flipped her wig. Literally. Hazel launched at Char and yanked her hair right off of her head."

I blink at her. "Are you telling me...?"

"That not one, but two old biddies in town want a piece of our boss? Yes. Yes, I am."

I press a hand to my stomach. "There are some things a person just doesn't need to know. You know?"

Kelly bursts out laughing. "Right? I'm never going to be able to look at him again without imagining—"

"Stop!" I hold up a hand and scrunch up my face. "Oh god. Too late."

Kelly rolls with another round of laughter just as the buzzer sounds at the front of the store, indicating a new shopper.

"I'll finish this up," Kelly offers, still giggling as she takes the broom and dustpan from me.

"Thanks." I head back to the only checkout lane that's open at this time of night, hoping it's neither Char or Hazel, because I just can't right now.

Fortunately, it's none other than my handsome cowboy.

"Hey, darlin'," he says as he saunters my way, looking like a sight for sore eyes. I think I secretly knew what he did for a living the first night he walked into Pony Up, because that sexy swagger of his is one-hundred-percent bull rider.

"Hey yourself. You look like you were working." I toe up for a quick kiss as he leans down for one.

"Sandy over at Magnolia Blue needed a hand with some things, so I offered to go since Wilder was busy taking cattle to Billings."

"Ah. Is her foreman still giving her grief?"

"Nah, not really. They've come to an understanding. Doesn't seem like such a bad guy once you get to know him."

"Well, that's good." I'm also dying to know if he talked to Cory, but I won't ask. As much as I want to make all of this easier on him, Holden is a big boy and this thing with Cory… it's between them, not me.

Besides, I need to save my energy for the bull riding battle, because that's something I'm not willing to give up on.

"Have you had dinner? I don't have much upstairs, but I'm done in an hour and we can grab something…" I thumb over my shoulder as he tucks his hands into his pockets.

"Actually, that's why I'm here. I'm going to cook for you tonight. And then we're going to watch a movie."

"Oh, we are?"

"Yep." His grin is so boyish and distracting that I almost miss the ambulance flying by outside.

"That's never a good sign." We don't get many emergency calls in Mason Creek, but when we do, they're almost always followed by bad news.

"I'm sure it's nothing. Someone probably fell down drunk at the bar or something."

I shake my head. "They're going in the wrong direction for that."

Holden lifts my chin and presses a kiss to my forehead. "It could literally be anything, babe. Now, let's talk about dinner. I'm actually a pretty shitty cook, so I was thinking grilled cheese, tomato soup, and ice cream for dessert."

"Only if it's the new coffee flavored stuff we just got in."

"Deal." He taps his finger on my nose and grabs a hand-basket before heading toward the soup aisle. I, being the opportunist that I am, unabashedly ogle his ass in those semi-snug Wranglers.

Maybe I don't want him going back to the rodeo after all.

"*TWILIGHT*? ARE YOU SERIOUS?"

"Yep." Holden gives a single nod, a smirk the size of Texas spreading across his handsome face as he turns off the soup and takes down two bowls. "As your boyfriend, it's my job to help you eradicate this fear of yours."

"And how do you figure watching a movie that depicts vampires living among us is going to help?"

"Ah, have you seen Robert Pattinson before, darlin'?" He makes an exasperated face and I roll my eyes.

"I don't believe for a second you've actually watched *Twilight*. And even if you did, you don't strike me as the kind of guy who'd know who played who."

He stares me down, trying his darnedest to look disappointed that I don't believe him, before he bursts out laughing. "Okay, fine. I've never actually watched the whole thing through, but my sister is a big fan and I've gleaned some background over the years."

"That's more like it." I wrinkle up my nose and grab the plates with our grilled cheese sandwiches, leading the way to the living room while he carries the soup.

He scarfs down two sandwiches by the time I can even get Netflix cued up on the TV.

And then there's a knock at the door.

We exchange confused looks, because no one ever visits. And more to the point, no one should have the code.

"I'll get it." Holden gets to his feet, brushing crumbs from his pants as he goes.

The ambulance screaming through town earlier comes to mind just as Holden opens the door and Aiden fills the empty space.

Holden told me about their conversation earlier, so I know he isn't here to cause problems, but the sullen look on his face says that whatever did bring him here isn't good news.

"Why do you look like someone died?" I ask bluntly, and the flicker of emotion that passes over his face makes my stomach turn. Oh god. Someone did die.

He shuffles slowly into the living room and drops down onto the couch next to where I sit on the floor, his MCSO baseball cap in his hands.

"Aiden, just tell me. It's not Mom or Dad, right? Because someone would have called—"

He shakes his head and when he speaks, his voice is hoarse. "Mom and Dad are fine. It's…" He trails off, rubbing a hand over his dark hair. "It's Marty, Al. He, uh, he didn't make it."

Just like that, my ears begin to ring and everything in my body feels like it's being pulled out of me on a slingshot. My vision goes white and then the slingshot launches and a million memories of Marty fly through my mind.

Coming into the market with my mom as a kid. Marty sneaking penny candy to me when we would check out. My job interview in high school. My job interview when I quit Montana State and came back to Mason Creek. The way he always called me kiddo, no matter how old I got or how much responsibility he gave me at the store.

That I loved him like a grandfather and never told him.

## CHAPTER 21

ALANA

*T*he next three days pass in a complete fog. Between the market and the gossiping customers, my calls with Marty's nephew and planning a funeral, I didn't even realize it was Tuesday afternoon until Holden called Susie in to close up and demanded I punch out.

"But I have so much to do," I protest as he hands me my purse and slings my backpack over his shoulder. "I have payroll to finish and the rodeo is this weekend and everyone will be coming to pick up their orders…"

"Alana," he says firmly, while gently but purposefully steering me toward the back of the store. "You haven't slept or eaten more than a container of yogurt in two days. I'm feeding you and putting you to bed, and you will not argue with me about it. Do you understand?"

"But who's going to—"

"Susie is capable of handling the store and the orders, and between Hallie and Emma, payroll will be taken care of, too. You're officially off the clock for at least the next few days."

"Days?" I shout. Or I think it's my voice anyway. My head is pounding so loud, it's hard to say.

Holden stops at the bottom of the stairs that lead to our apartment and grasps my shoulders. "Babe, if you don't stop and take care of yourself, Marty's won't be the only funeral in Mason Creek this week."

"Oh."

"Uh huh. Now come on, let's get you upstairs."

The next thing I comprehend is Holden pulling a sheet over me in bed. Sun still shines through the window, but I'm in my pajamas and my belly no longer feels like it's eating itself.

"Lie down with me?" I whisper, and he nods.

The last thing I remember is burying my face in his chest and finally letting myself cry.

---

"He loved you like a daughter," Tucker Simms says when it's his turn in the receiving line after the funeral on Wednesday. "He used to come into the auto shop just to shoot the shit, and he always talked about what a good job you were doing with the store. Said he would have sold the place years ago if it hadn't been for you."

"Thank you, Tucker." I give him a hug, knowing he meant his words to be comforting. He couldn't possibly know that they're actually the very last ones I want to hear today. Or ever.

"How are you doing, sweetie? Can I get you something to drink?" My mom sneaks into line while Sadie's parents share their sympathies with Dalton and his wife Brittany.

"No, I'm good, but thank you." Only a handful of people remain in the line and then I'll have a few minutes to regroup before we head to the cemetery and then the traditional funeral potluck at the town hall.

Holden rubs circles on my back and leans down to press a kiss to my temple. "You're doing great, babe. Just a couple more hours to go."

"Yeah," I squeak out, but the truth is, I'm not sure I'll feel any better in a couple hours. I'm not sure I'll feel better in a week or even a month.

Dalton and Brittany want to sell the Mason Creek Market. They told me as much this morning when they arrived from Idaho. They have two middle school children and a business of their own, and they don't have time or interest in owning a grocery store a whole state away.

Which means there's a chance I could be out of a job before too long. I can't afford to buy the store and there's no guarantee that whoever does will want to keep me on.

Oh, and... I'm probably going to have to find a new place to live. So, there's that, as well.

"Oh, Alana, I am so sorry." Sadie's mom, Cybill, breaks down as soon as she steps in front of me. She clasps my hands and her entire body shakes as her husband Burt moves to stand beside her, looking as red-faced as his wife but without the tears, and we all know why.

"You have to know that she never meant any harm," Cybill continues on. "She was just... well, you know what happened, dear. Who would have thought?"

Who would have thought Granny Char would have ridden Marty off into his last sunset? I don't think a single person in town saw that one coming—no pun intended— except for maybe Hazel Jackson.

"I know," I tell Cybill, patting her hand. I have no other words. Aside from, "I hope she doesn't blame herself."

For some reason, that makes Cybill sob even harder. Burt

just shrugs and passes me an apologetic frown as he ushers her out of the church.

"At least no one's talking about our ride anymore," Holden mutters beside me and it's all I can do not to collapse in a fit of laughter and tears.

---

"To Old Man Morton," Wilder says that evening as we gather in his and Hallie's kitchen with wine and the biggest taco bar I've ever seen, thanks to Emma, who couldn't make it any more obvious she's eating for two. "For the friendship, the memories, and for giving this town something to talk about for the next seventy-six years."

An assortment of laughs, snorts, and 'to Marty' fill the room followed by the clinking of glasses and a mad dash for the food.

My appetite still isn't what it should be, but I manage to eat two tacos before I head out to the front porch and claim one of the big wooden chairs.

Wilder joins me a few minutes later, and we sit in silence for what feels like hours before he finally speaks.

"Hallie told me that Marty's nephew wants to sell."

I nod. "I figured he would."

"Me too. Mason Creek is a small town and it's hard for outsiders to see the value we see in it, you know?"

"All too well." My gaze drifts to the mountain set aglow by the setting sun, and I sigh.

"Let me loan you the down payment."

My eyes snap back to Wilder. "Excuse me?"

"I know you want to buy the place, Al. And you've worked too damn hard not to do it."

"I could never ask you—"

"You're not asking, I'm offering." He presses his lips into a sincere smile. "In case you didn't know, Levi and I run a pretty successful ranch out here. I don't mind sharing my good fortune, especially with someone I know is as invested in this town as I am."

"Wilder..." My eyes fill with tears and I'm at a loss for words. I open my mouth to try and say something. To tell him no, to thank him... I don't know. I'm just so freaking blown away. So grateful.

The door creaks open beside me and Hallie steps out with her cell phone in hand. She looks from Wilder to me and back again, and he nods.

"I told her," he says. "I think she's still processing."

Hallie smiles. "That's okay. You don't have to decide now. In fact..." She glances down at her phone. "Maybe you should wait a bit."

Wilder and I both frown, and then the sound of tires crunching on gravel in the driveway interrupts.

"What in the hell?" Wilder gets to his feet, a confused look on his face as two car doors shut.

I can't see around him, so I get to my feet as well, just as Brayden, Hallie's boss at the bank, and Simon Wright, one of the lawyers in town, start up the porch steps.

"Wilder, Hallie," Brayden says before he offers me a small smile and his hand. "Alana, I'm sorry to hear about Marty."

"T-thank you. It was certainly unexpected." Kind of like him showing up like this, with Simon, no less.

Brayden nods and Hallie holds up a finger. "Let me grab Holden."

Simon takes a seat in the empty chair beside me, and it's then that I realize he's holding a manila folder.

Oh my god, Dalton is evicting me. I haven't paid rent and Marty and I never even had a rental agreement. I won't be able to fight this. And Holden... he'll have to find someplace else to stay, too.

Hallie returns with Holden behind her. He glances around, the crease in his brow deepening.

"What's going on here?" he asks, resting his hand on the back of my chair.

"I think we're being evicted," I rasp, trying desperately not to cry.

"What?" Holden demands. "She's busted her ass for that store and Dalton wants to kick her out?"

"We're not here to evict you," Brayden says, holding up a hand. "Quite the opposite, in fact."

Simon sits forward, opens the folder, and then hands me two sheets of paper.

A letter from Marty…

And the deed to the Mason Creek Market.

# CHAPTER 22

HOLDEN

"*I* can't believe he left me everything."

I grin at Alana, turning in circles in the middle of Marty's living room on Friday morning. Not only did he leave her the store, he left her his house and the majority of his savings, too. Aside from a little college money for Dalton's children, Marty's will, updated just six months ago, listed Alana as primary beneficiary.

The letter that accompanied it all was short and to the point, yet it said so much.

*Dear Alana,*

*My Myrtle and I never had children of our own, and I never regretted that decision until Myrtle moved on to the big Montana sky and left me all alone.*

*When you showed up and became a part of my life, you helped fill that void. You are a bright, beautiful, independent woman, and if I ever had a daughter, I'd have wanted her to be just like you.*

*Keep making me proud, kiddo.*

*Love,*
*Marty*

"Do you think you'll move in here?" I ask, glancing around at the modest bungalow. It's outdated but well kept, and the scent of cigars and old books pairs well with the vintage pictures on the walls and the kitschy knickknacks on the shelves. "I mean, it's definitely your style."

She half laughs, half snorts. "Totally me." Then in a more serious tone, "I don't think I could live here. I also don't think I could sell it, either. That doesn't feel right. I suppose I have some time to think about it."

I nod. "We'll have to winterize it, but we've got plenty of time for that."

"We?" She arches an eyebrow above one of those gorgeous eyes and I can't help but pull her to me.

"We're a *we*, babe, and will be indefinitely if I have anything to say about it. Better get used to that." I kiss the tip of her nose, and she makes a scrunched up face.

"You're kinda bossy, Colorado."

"Gotta keep up with you, darlin'."

She rolls her eyes and lifts my arm to check the time on my watch. "We should get going. I have some things to get together for the rodeo tonight."

"I thought Susie and Nancy were manning the market's booth."

"They are, but I told them the very least I could do was set up, since they're working all weekend."

"So, you're free then, right? To enjoy the festivities with me?"

She smiles, but her hesitation is as apparent as those freckles on her cheeks. "Of course."

"You'll hate every second of it, won't you?"

"It's not that I hate the rodeo…" She sighs. "In fact, I used to love it."

"Until Cory."

She nods. "Yeah. He kind of ruined it for me."

I tighten my arms around her. "How long has it been since you've gone?"

"More than four years," she admits and there's an undercurrent of sadness in her tone. Like maybe she's missed it more than she's allowed herself to admit.

"What are the chances I'd be able to talk you into going with me?"

She laughs and the prettiest pink stains her cheeks. "I don't know…"

"Come on, darlin', I can't have my girlfriend hating what I do for a living."

Her brows lift. "What you do, present tense. Does that mean you're not quitting?"

"It means I haven't made my mind up yet."

A satisfied smile spreads across her lips. "Okay. I'll take that for now."

"I'm riding this weekend."

Her eyes go wide and her mouth drops open. "Are you serious?"

I nod, and she jumps up into my arms, her excitement bursting.

"Have you been holding out on me all this time, Holden Daniel?"

I laugh. "When I heard the rodeo was coming to town, I was kinda hoping the assault stuff would be old news so I could have some fun."

"The timing is perfect!" She bounces up again and smacks her lips to mine only to pull back abruptly. Her whiskey eyes dart back and forth between mine for a long moment, before she swallows. "Is Cory going to be there, too?"

"I don't know." When I talked to him last Saturday after the blowup at Pony Up, he wasn't sure he wanted to stick around town any longer than he had to. He went off about everyone in Mason Creek hating him because of Alana, and when I pointed out that they probably hated him because he treated her like shit, he got real quiet. "But if I keep riding, he's going to be around. We can't avoid him forever."

She's thoughtful for another beat and then she pulls her shoulders back and lifts her chin. "I want to support you more than I want to avoid him. And I can't very well push you to keep riding and not be your biggest fan, now can I?"

"You've never seen me on a bull, babe. I might suck."

"You've missed three events and you're still sixth overall in points, Colorado. I'm pretty sure you don't suck."

"I thought we agreed you weren't going to look me up."

"And I thought you weren't going to connive with my coworkers behind my back anymore."

I blink down at her. "I have no idea what you're talking about."

"Uh huh." She pokes at my chest. "I know you sweet-talked Susie and Nancy into covering the whole weekend so I wouldn't have to, even though it's my job now."

"Don't be too mad, babe. I just wanted the opportunity to hopefully make you love the rodeo again. Maybe make you proud, too."

"I'm already proud of you, cowboy."

"Just wait until you see me in action."

Her grin stretches wide, and if her looking up at me like that is my reward, I might just keep riding bulls after all.

ALANA

"That's him, huh? I can see why you held out on me." The familiar voice sounds behind me as I watch Holden talk animatedly with a bunch of the rodeo company's staff by the gates.

"Get your eyes off my man, Mads." I turn to my best friend with a grin and arms ready for a hug.

"But he's so cute!" she squeals as she launches herself at me. "And between you and me, he fills out those Wranglers very nicely."

"Oh my god." I laugh. "You and your cowboys."

"Me?" She pulls back, her eyes sparkling as she takes me in. "You're the one who went and fell in love with one!"

"I'm not—"

"You so are. And it looks damn good on you, too." She purses her lips and gives me another once-over. "You holding up okay with everything else going on?"

I nod. "For the most part. I think I'm still in shock, but the store has kept me so busy that I haven't had time to dwell on it."

"And your classes? How are they going?"

"Good. I'm so glad I only have the two right now. How about you, Ms. Master's Degree?"

A bright grin splits across her face. "I have an interview with Nash & Broadfield next week."

"Mads!" I throw my arms around her for another hug. "That's awesome!" She's had her heart set on a position at the big architectural engineering firm for years now, and she'd bided her time, waiting until she was further along in her degree. "I have no doubt you'll nail it."

She lifts her shoulder, a sheepish blush creeping into her cheeks. "Here's hoping, anyway."

I give her a playful poke, then wrap my arm around her waist and lead her back to the gate where I've been watching the rodeo team finalize everything for tonight's performance. Kickoff is in two hours and a few spectators have already arrived to claim seats in the stands.

"So, you mentioned something about him not going back on the road," Madelyn says as we watch Holden shake hands with another guy on the other side of the arena. They're clearly friends, given the half hug that follows.

"He's undecided." And the more I see him in his element like this, the more I know it's where he belongs.

"And if he goes back? How will you feel about that?"

"I'll miss him, but I don't want to hold him back, either."

She nods and watches for another minute. "You could hire a new manager for the store, and I don't know, go on the road with him? Maybe have a life for once?"

I laugh. "For one, I have a life. And two, he travels with Cory."

"I like how you didn't say no." My friend smirks. "Anyway, how are you handling *that*? Him being one of Cory's besties and all."

"Cory and I haven't said more than twenty words to each other in nearly four years. My concern was more about how Holden would feel, and he said being with me is more important." I shrug, even though saying those words— knowing he feels that way—is anything but insignificant.

"Speaking of the cheating jerk…" Madelyn lifts her chin to the right where Cory approaches Holden and the other guys, his vest hanging from his hand.

Ah, so he is riding this weekend. "I wasn't sure he'd show up."

"I hope he draws the meanest bull and gets his dick stomped on, too."

"He wears a cup."

"Quit ruining my fun."

HOLDEN

"Two ABR superstars at our little rodeo? Well, I'll be damned." Dean, the foreman from the Magnolia Blue Ranch, extends his hand to Cory.

"Figured it was time I gave the home crowd a little show." He chuckles and flicks a smug grin my way. "You riding too, lover boy, or are you just here to look pretty and sign autographs?"

I shoot him a wink. "By the time we're done this weekend, you'll be wanting one, too."

His smirk hitches a little higher to one side. "Awfully cocky for someone who hasn't ridden in almost a month, don't you think?"

"A month full of pent-up resentment," I remind him. I'm not going down tonight without a fight. Especially not to him.

He scoffs. "Yeah, well, we'll see how that works out for you."

Watching us with an arched eyebrow, Dean clears his throat. "Looks like they've opened up registration."

Cory digs his boots into the dirt and strides toward the table without another word.

"I know you pro guys are hella competitive, but I get the feeling there's something more going on here," Dean mutters as we follow after.

"Eh. Mitchell doesn't like losing, that's all."

But that's exactly what's going to happen this weekend if I have anything to say about it, because this win isn't just about flipping off my accuser and the ABR...

I want to win for my girl, too.

## ALANA

"I think I'm going to be sick." I press my hand to my stomach as the first night of bronc competition wraps up and the announcer amps up the crowd for the final event of the night—the bulls.

Madelyn just smiles. "You forgot about that part, huh?"

"Unfortunately." This is always the part of the night where the excitement turns to anxiety, and all of the worst-case scenarios come to mind. Will he hang on? Will his bull be tough enough to score well, but not so tough that he ends up hurt? What if he does get hurt? Will it be a bad injury?

And because I've never been to one of Holden's events before, I have a whole other set of questions. Will he want me by his side if he's injured? What if he has to go to the hospital? Did he list me as an emergency contact?

My mind is racing, all for a ride that'll be over in eight seconds.

From the bleachers behind me, Wilder clasps his hands on my shoulders and leans down to be heard above the music. "You wanna place bets on his score?"

"You think he'll hang on?"

Wilder nods. "Without a doubt. He's got a score to settle."

I bite my lip. "That's what I'm afraid of."

"It's what he does, Al. It's in his blood. And he's damn good at it, too."

"I'm going with seventy-five," Madelyn chimes in, as Jake Owen's "Eight Second Ride" begins to play over the speakers and the rodeo clowns toss T-shirts into the crowd.

"Only seventy-five?" I scoff. How dare she doubt my man.

Hallie laughs. "I guess you're not that worried."

"I'll take eighty," Wilder says.

"I've got eighty-one," Hallie adds, sticking her tongue out at Wilder.

I glance back to the arena, catching a glimpse of him shrugging his vest behind the gates and the chute.

He looks up as if he feels me watching and winks.

"Ninety," I say boldly. "And I'm calling a shiny new buckle by the time this weekend is over, too."

HOLDEN

Bermuda is easily the orneriest beast in the trailers this weekend, so of course I drew him.

Cory laughed, Dean grimaced, and I held my head high, knowing damn well that a rowdy bull could pay off big on the scoreboard. He could very well break my back, too, but that's a risk I take every time I strap up.

Seven riders have already gone and only one made eight. Dean is in the chute now and I hold my breath as he gives the nod and the gate opens. His bull, Mad Dog, goes right and then left, bucking to beat hell, but not with the ferocity needed to put up a big score. Still, Dean holds on and the crowd goes wild. Seventy-four points later, he's in the lead with Cory on deck.

He rides like the pro he is and scores an eighty-nine.

Dammit. I'll need that coveted ninety to beat him. I've topped it plenty of times before, but the stakes have never felt higher than they do tonight.

My girl is in the crowd and my career is in limbo. I want to win as a means of thanking her for believing in me and to prove to myself that this is where I belong.

"You're up, McMurray." One of the guys waves me over and I pop in my mouth guard.

The adrenaline pumps through my veins as I bounce on my toes, crane my head from side to side, and then stride toward the chute like I've done hundreds of times before.

"He's already good and pissed for you," one of the handlers says as I climb the gate and hover above the massive white bull. Bermuda grunts and stomps and thrashes the second he feels me settle down, working the strap around my gloved right hand.

"Good," I mutter under my breath, making sure the leather is nice and snug. "That's how I like 'em."

Then I give my nod and the gate swings open.

Bermuda isn't just pissed, he's friggin' enraged. His rear end whips around like a damn tornado, tossing my ass and arm in the air like they're nothing. But I hang on and I hang on some more until the buzzer sounds. When I slip from the bull, hitting the arena floor in a cloud of dust, the crowd is on their feet.

The announcer sings my praises and the guys whistle and call out from behind the gate, but it's the grin on Alana's face and the tears in her eyes that mean the most.

"You did it!" I hear her scream above the crowd, as she jumps up and down, her hands pressed together like a prayer in front of that pretty smile.

And then the announcer's voice sounds over the loud-speaker once again and I can tell she's holding her breath right along with me.

"And that's a ninety-one point, folks. The top score of the night and a new Mason Creek rodeo record."

"That's my man!" she hoots and then takes off for the staging area.

I run out of the arena, too, and we damn near collide on the dirt path out back.

"Halfway to that buckle, baby!" She jumps into my arms and crashes her mouth to mine while I stick my hat on her head and spin her around.

"I don't need the buckle, darlin'. I already won with you." She laughs and I'm pretty sure it's the prettiest sound I've ever heard.

---

I RIDE AGAIN on Saturday and with a single point over Cory, the silver buckle and the Mason Creek rodeo title is mine.

"So, now what?" Alana asks after the big win. "Do you still want to quit something you're so obviously meant to do?"

I shake my head, knowing she was right all along. "I think I have to finish what I started."

"Damn right, you do." She toes up and her kiss is like fuel on an already blazing fire. "Go get 'em, cowboy."

# CHAPTER 23

ALANA

"*I* miss you, darlin'."

"I miss you more." I tuck my hands between my cheek and my pillow while gazing at my phone propped against Holden's. Unfortunately, the handsome face looking back at me is confined to a screen for thirteen more days.

"I doubt that. I swear I wake up thinking about you and I can't fall asleep at night until we do this."

"You should be exhausted." He's been back on the road for a month now, and he's hit every event, riding his heart out in hopes of landing the top five going into the world finals at the end of October.

"I am, but it's not the same sleeping without you."

"You've done it for twenty-seven years without me, cowboy."

"Worst twenty-seven years of my life."

I laugh, and from his travel trailer parked somewhere in Nebraska, Holden grins.

"Have you started packing for Vegas yet?"

"I have three and a half weeks. If I pack now, I'll have nothing to wear."

He arches an eyebrow. "You wearing those little dresses for someone else?"

"Stop!" I laugh so hard, the phone flips over. When I prop it up again, he's on his back, holding his phone above him. His chest is bare and full of lean, sun-kissed muscle, and my mouth goes dry. "Really? You have to taunt me?"

"Just making sure you remember what you've got, so you don't go finding someone to replace me while I'm gone."

"You don't play fair."

"All is fair in love and war, babe."

I roll my eyes, but my heart hiccups at the mention of a certain four-lettered L word. We've been together for almost two months now and there isn't a doubt in my mind that every bit of me is in love with every bit of him, but I can't tell him over the phone. When I finally tell him how I feel, I plan to kiss the heck out of him, too.

"You have nothing to worry about and you know it."

"What about that guy from the café? What was his name again? Cody?"

"Cole."

"See!" He laughs. "You knew exactly who I was talking about!"

"Because he was literally the only person we ever talked to at Wren's."

"Uh huh." He shakes his head and blows out a breath, just as there's a knock on his end of the line. "Hold on a minute, babe." Then, "Yeah?"

There's a voice on the other end of the line, but I can't make out what's being said. Probably for the best anyway, since I'm sure it's Cory.

Things are still tense between them, but they're doing their best, knowing the season will wrap up soon. Holden hasn't confirmed whether or not he'll tour again next year, but he did renew his ABR membership, so he hasn't ruled it out, either.

"Babe, I gotta go. Apparently we're reviewing footage from last night's rides again." He gives me an apologetic frown, and as sad as I always am when it's time to hang up, I smile and blow him a kiss.

"Have fun, babe. And don't forget I'm going to a barn dance at Magnolia Blue with Hallie and Wilder tomorrow night."

He nods. "Thank you for that, by the way. I feel bad that I can't be there to congratulate Sandy on the sale, so make sure she knows you're there for me, too."

"Of course." We blow each other a few more kisses, say goodbye a half dozen more times, and finally hang up ten minutes later.

And like the crazy person I am, I pull out my homework, because what I didn't tell Holden is that I can't sleep without him, either.

---

"Oh, my gosh, look at this place!" Hallie rushes ahead into the big, beautiful red barn nestled near what Wilder told us was the original homestead, long before the property became the Magnolia Blue Ranch.

Thousands of white twinkling lights adorn the rafters and beams, while hay bales, cornstalks, pumpkins, dried sunflowers, and fresh, colorful mums adorn the rest of the place. It's a gorgeous, festive scene. Romantic even.

The only thing missing is a handsome cowboy to hold my hand.

"I feel like someone took a peek at my preteen diary," I sigh, spinning in a circle to take it all in. "Because this is how

I've envisioned my wedding reception ever since I was a little girl."

Wilder rolls his eyes and tucks his hands into his jeans. "You had to go there, huh? Now Hal's gonna be talking about what she wants at our wedding all night."

Hallie nods. "You got that right."

I point a stern finger at him. "Better give this lady what she wants, Wilder. She puts up with a lot from you."

Poor guy doesn't even try to look offended. Just shrugs and wraps his arm around Hallie when she snuggles close.

We arrived right on time, but most of the tables along the side of the makeshift dance floor are already occupied, so I gesture to a vacant one near where the band is set up.

"Might be a little loud, but it's better than in front of the bar where we'll probably end up wearing a few drinks."

"Perfect!" Hallie tugs Wilder toward the table when I spot Holden's friend Dean across the way. He's talking with a couple of younger guys dressed in cowboy boots and their best pearl snap shirts, but when he spots me, he raises his drink and waves me over.

"I'm going to talk to Dean. I'll be right back," I tell my friends before heading over, careful that the cool fall breeze dancing through the open barn doors doesn't catch my dress and cause a scene.

"Hey there, gorgeous." Dean is all smiles and even pecks my cheek in greeting. He's a little older than Holden, probably around Wilder's age, and his vibe is one-hundred-percent big brother rather than big flirt.

He gestures to the younger men, all gussied up for the night. "Alana, this is Ryder and his brother Aaron. They're both ranch hands here at Magnolia Blue. Boys, this is Alana Faulkner, Holden McMurray's girl. She's also the new owner of the grocery store over in Mason Creek."

Both of the men seem surprised and then Ryder clears his

throat as he offers his hand. "Nice to meet you, ma'am."

I laugh. "Oh, no no. None of that ma'am stuff. I'm not much older than either of you."

They both blush and then quickly excuse themselves when a group of young women enters the barn.

Dean takes a pull from his beer and then realizes my hands are empty. "Shoot, you need a drink, girl. Let me grab you something."

He tips his head toward the bar and I follow, the sound of my boots on the hardwood muted out when the twang of a guitar and the vibration of cymbals fills the air before the band starts the night off with a country classic.

"Wow, they're pretty good," I say to Dean while we wait for my bottle of hard cider.

"Yep, and they're local, too. I think one of the guys used to play with Tucker Simms." The bartender hands my drink to Dean, who passes it to me before tucking some cash into a big cup on the makeshift bar. "It's on the house tonight, so don't be shy."

"Ah. I don't drink much, but thanks for the heads-up." I tip my bottle toward his.

"No problem." We clink glass and he leans back against the bar. "So, I heard Holden got a ninety-one last weekend in Santa Fe."

Pride blooms in my chest. "It was an amazing ride." One I wish I'd been able to see in person, but the up close and personal video he'd shared was at least better than the one I'd seen on TV.

"He's a damn good bull rider. I don't know what all happened with him or why he was in Mason Creek when he was, but I'm glad to see him back at it."

"Me too." As much as I miss him, the rodeo is where he belongs. "Vegas can't come soon enough."

"You going down for the championship?" he asks.

"I am. I'm excited and terrified at the same time." Holden doesn't have enough points to win the overall, but he could take the final event and that's almost as good.

He chuckles and lifts his beer. "Welcome to bull riding."

I grin, too, and then glance around. "So, where is Sandy? I haven't met her yet and I'm supposed to send congratulations from Holden."

Dean smirks. "She was outside talking with the future owner, but she should be coming in soon."

"The future owner? I thought the ranch was already sold."

"It's practically a done deal. Just waiting on closing, which takes a little longer with property like this. Shouldn't be a problem though. Credible guy and whatnot."

"Ah, okay. Will you point her out when you see her or send her my way? This place is really filling up fast and I don't want to fail my mission."

He dips his chin as the band rolls into another song—the Grundy County Auction one—which is basically impossible not to dance to. The mad dash of people lining up on the dance floor proves it.

"You feel like tearing it up?" Dean asks, quickly finishing off his drink.

I hesitate only because my drink is still full, but he seems to recognize my predicament.

"Here…" He plucks it from my hand and sets it in front of an elderly couple sharing a plateful of barbecue and potato salad. "Mrs. J, if you could keep an eye on this pretty lady's drink, we'd be forever grateful."

Then, before I can argue, I'm in the middle of a line dance, nailing moves I haven't tried in years. Funny how these come back to us so easily.

By the time the song ends and a much slower one begins, I'm lightheaded and wishing I had a bottle of water instead of a hard cider.

I sway a little on my feet as I head toward Mrs. J., and before I can reach out for one of the lighted beams to catch my balance, an arm slides around my waist.

"Whoa, darlin'. Don't need you passing out on me before I can properly kiss you hello."

The voice, the scent, the lips against my ear… They turn me to absolute goo right there in the middle of the Magnolia Blue barn.

He chuckles softly when I let myself sag against him for just a moment before I spin and everything in my world is right again.

"What on earth are you doing here?" I cup his face, noting his beard is a little thicker in person than it appeared on video, and press my mouth to his in a long, breathtaking kiss before he can answer.

"Wow," he says when we finally break apart. "You weren't lying when you said you missed me."

"I never lie to you," I sigh, brushing my nose against his. "But it seems you can't say the same. Aren't you supposed to be in Nebraska?"

With his arms locked around my waist, he rocks me from side to side with a mischievous glint in his eyes. "I *was* in Nebraska. Until Brent knocked on my door last night and told me he was going to leave me there if I didn't quit sweet-talking my girl and get in his damn truck."

"Why didn't you tell me you were coming?" I shove at his chest and he just grins a little wider.

"Have you met Sandy yet? Or were you too busy dancing with Dean?"

I roll my eyes. "Line dancing, you goof."

"I see you wore one of my dresses." Hands on my hips, he pushes me away to get a better look. "Fuck, you're sexy. I'd be pissed except for I already have plans for what I'm going to do to you as soon as I can get you alone in one of these dark corners."

Heat fills my cheeks and other parts of my body, as well."

"The only thing I don't like is this." He tugs at my denim jacket and then leans down to my ear. "I can't see how hard your nipples are."

Dark corners. Where is the nearest dark corner?

"I felt that shiver, darlin'. And I fully intend to find out what you're hiding, but there are a couple people I want you to meet first. Come on."

My head spinning from his unexpected appearance and then his wicked promises, I let him lead me toward the front of the barn where I spot Wilder and Hallie talking with an older woman and two older men.

"McMurray." Wilder claps Holden on the back. "Good to see you."

"Thanks for looking after my girl while I was gone." Holden slides an arm around my shoulders and kisses my temple, before turning to the older woman. "Alana, I'd like you to meet Sandy Wagner, the soon-to-be former owner of Magnolia Blue."

"Oh, I'm so glad to finally meet you," the older woman coos. "Holden's told me so much about you."

He has? "Likewise. Holden really enjoyed helping you when he was here in Montana."

She smiles kindly but says no more, so Holden moves on.

"And this is my Uncle Miles." He gestures to the taller of the two men, both of whom are dressed in blue jeans, flannel shirts, and dark Stetsons.

"Ah, Alana. You're even prettier than your pictures."

My pictures? Okay, this is getting weird. "Um, thank you."

Finally, Holden takes a step forward and shifts me to stand in front of him. "And this is my dad, Wyatt."

His dad? I'm meeting his father without any warning?

He's definitely going to hear about this later.

The older man, who has the same kind, dark eyes as Holden not only takes my hand but pulls me in for a hug. "His mama is gonna be so mad that I got to meet you first, so maybe let's not tell her, eh?"

I laugh, already liking this guy a whole lot. "I won't say anything if you won't."

He chuckles as he lets go, and Holden tucks me back into his side.

"So, you're probably wondering why we're here," Miles says, smiling almost secretively at Holden, and that's when it dawns on me.

"Oh my gosh, you're buying Magnolia Blue." Holden's told me all about his uncle's ranch in Colorado. How his dad has been the foreman for years and that they're some of the best ranchers he's ever known.

Miles shakes his head as Holden clears his throat.

"Actually, I'm buying Magnolia."

It takes a full ten seconds for his words to register.

"Excuse m-me?" I sputter, because surely I've heard him wrong.

"Nothing is final until we close the first part of November, but, yes, darlin'. Magnolia Blue is going to be mine. Well, mine with a small investment from Uncle Miles."

The ground beneath my feet begins to move again, but Holden is right there, like the savior he's been from the very start.

"Let's find a place to sit, darlin'," he says all but scooping me off of my feet.

"Good idea. You two go and catch up and then come find us in the barn. I'd like a dance with my future daughter-in-law before I head back to Colorado." Wyatt winks, and if it weren't for Holden's tight grip on my side, I'd think I was dreaming.

"Here," Holden says a minute later, urging me to sit on a small bench beside an outbuilding that's set back from the barn and away from guests. "Do you need something to drink? Water or—"

"You bought a ranch in Montana." I blink up at him and he nods. "Sit and explain this to me."

"I know it's a lot to take in." He lowers down to the bench and removes his cowboy hat to push a hand through his hair. "I wanted to surprise you, but I'm starting to think that was a bad idea. You're not mad—"

"Why on earth would I be mad?" I turn to him, unable to keep the grin from my face or the tears from my eyes.

"Because I want you to live here with me and I haven't even told you I love you yet."

"You love me?" I rasp, and he tips his head toward the moonlit mountains rising above the river in the distance.

"I love you bigger than those mountains, brighter than that moon, and stronger than that river, darlin'."

"Holden…" I cry his name as he pulls me onto his lap.

"I know the past couple of months have been crazy, and you didn't even like me when we first met. But we've been through some trying times together. My suspension, Marty passing, figuring out everything with the store, me going back on the road…" He tucks a lock of hair behind my ear and his fingers linger on my skin. "But I think we did a damn good job being there for each other, and if I'm honest, I don't think I could have done it without you."

"I feel the same," I say, swiping at my tears. "I had no idea I needed you until you showed up at my door. I tried to resist the pull I felt toward you, because I haven't needed anyone in a very long time. But now…" I curl my hand around his stubbled jaw. "I not only need you, but I love you, too."

The corners of his mouth tug into the sexiest grin. "See, I knew you were getting sweet on me."

I laugh and he buries his face in my neck. "You really didn't have to buy a ranch in Montana to prove your point."

"No, but look at that view and tell me that isn't ours." He points across the pasture to the mountains once again. "That's you, me, and forever, darlin'."

It is beautiful and the picture he paints is more than I could have ever imagined. But… "What about bull riding?"

He pulls in a breath and nods. "You were right. I'm not ready to walk away."

Relief rushes through my veins and I smile.

"I'll have a few months off to get everything situated before the next season. Then Dean will take the lead on the day-to-day stuff, just like he's doing now. I'll be home as often as I can to check in and I'm kinda hoping you'll be here, too. Not to work, because I know you're tied up with the store, but just in case Dean needs someone to bounce stuff off of. And Wilder has offered to do what he can, too.

"But I only want to ride one more year. So I can end things on a season I have complete control over. A season I can give my all, and a season I can share with you."

My heart clenches. "I've already decided to hire a new manager at the store. I want to free up my schedule so I can catch a few of your shows."

His eyes light up. "I love you so friggin' much."

"And I love you." I wrap my arms around his neck and press my forehead to his. "What do you plan to do with all that extra time once you hang up those spurs?"

"That's easy, darlin'. I'm coming back to Montana and making you my wife."

I gasp. "Is that a proposal?"

He shakes his head. "Nope, not yet. But I already have it planned out."

I smile. "Another perfect secret?"

"The best one yet."

# EPILOGUE

*ONE YEAR LATER*

ALANA

"$\mathcal{H}$e did it. Holy crap, he really did it."

"Did you have any doubt, girlie?" Holden's dad slings an arm around my shoulder and gives me a quick squeeze.

"No, not really." I laugh. Holden's lead in points for the past five events and his determination to win only grew as the season went on.

"You know we're gonna hear about it for the rest of our lives, right?" Kaden, Holden's younger brother, gives an annoyed sigh. The gleam in his eyes, however, is pure pride.

"Aren't we supposed to head down now?" his mother asks, pointing to the side of the arena where they're staging for the post-event interviews and awards.

"How's my hair look?" Tessa, the baby of the McMurray family, ducks in front of me, fussing with her blonde locks. "Is my makeup okay?"

I smirk. "Better not let your brother see you primping for these cowboys."

She waggles her eyebrows. "I dare him to tell me I can't. I'm twenty-one now and plenty old enough."

Pretty sure she'll never be old enough in Holden's eyes, but who am I to tell her that?

We make our way down to the arena floor, flash our VIP passes, and are instantly met with congratulations and smiles from Holden's friends and the ABR staff.

"He killed it tonight, Al!" Brent lifts me off the ground for a big hug. "Did you see how he almost lost it around six-three, but somehow out-muscled that damn bull and held on?"

I laugh. "That's my man."

Brent just shakes his head in wonderment and sets me back down.

"Hands off my girl, Shaw." A sexy, possessive voice sounds in my ear before a big arm snakes around my waist.

Brent lifts his hands and takes a few steps back, grinning like a fool. "Just singing your praises, man."

Holden grunts and spins me to face him. He's sweaty and dirty and pure sex on two, leather-clad legs. "Told you I'd win, darlin'."

"Mmm hmm." That's all I say before I kiss the crap out of him. Behind us, someone—probably Kaden—groans.

"Save it for the hotel room, will ya?"

Holden chuckles and then a tall man with the biggest cowboy hat I've ever seen taps him on the shoulder.

"Time to roll, champ. You can bring your lady with you if you want."

"Damn right, I am." He threads his fingers with mine and leads the way toward the mass of people with cameras, microphones, and trophies gathered by the tunnel. The energy in the arena is magnetic and every single person we pass either claps him on the shoulder or shakes his hand.

I've shared this moment with him a couple of times already this season, but this level of excitement is on another level. This is the big time and tonight, all of the world is watching.

A broad-shouldered man with a mic shakes Holden's hand while another hands him a gigantic silver cup.

"Holden McMurray! How does it feel to be not only the winner here tonight in Las Vegas, but the new ABR world champion!" the man hollers the last four words and the crowd in the Coast2Coast Mobile Arena cheers as confetti floats through the air.

"It feels amazing, Jim!" Holden raises the massive trophy above his head and I've never been more proud of him in my life. He worked his butt off this year and he accomplished exactly what he set out to do.

"You won the title three years ago and then last year you took a break and we weren't sure we'd see you ride again," the big man says into the mic. "But you came back stronger than ever, and now you're taking the ABR championship home again. I'd say that's one hell of a comeback."

"Sure is. And I couldn't have done it without this lady right here." He wraps an arm around my shoulders as one of the other riders takes the trophy. "She pushed me to come back and keep doing what I love and I can't thank her enough for believing in me."

Tears fill my eyes and I can't look away from him.

"I told you once that you were better than any title and I still mean that. You are the ultimate prize, darlin', and I hope you'll let me be yours."

He drops to one knee in his vest and his chaps and his dusty cowboy hat, and time. Stands. Still.

He pulls a small black box from his pocket and flips it

open to reveal a gorgeous diamond ring that sparkles and shines beneath the stadium lights.

I cover my mouth with my hands as sob after sob bursts from my chest. He promised his proposal would be perfect, but I never expected this.

"Will you marry me, Alana Faulkner?" His dark eyes shine so brightly with love that's unmistakable even through my own tears.

"Yes." I hiccup and then laugh. "Yes, I'll marry you!"

He's on his feet in an instant, spinning me around once again, and all I can think about is how damn lucky I am. That he showed up on my doorstep and showed me how to love all over again.

And now I get to spend the rest of my life loving him even more.

"This night is going to be pretty hard to top," I say against his lips, and he grins.

"Oh, darlin', but I'm just getting started."

## THE END

Want more Mason Creek? Start back where it all began in
***Perfect Risk by C.A. Harms*** only on Amazon!

---

Sign up for my mailing list to keep up-to-date on all my book news, too! I'd love to have you my Facebook reader group, as well!
**https://www.mollymclain.com/newsletter**
Search for **Molly's Misfits (Molly McLain's Reader Group)**
on Facebook!

---

**And how about the rest of the Mason Creek books?**

Here's the full list of books on Kindle Unlimited!

Perfect Risk by C.A Harms
Perfect Song by Lauren Runow
Perfect Love by A.M. Hargrove
Perfect Night by Terri E. Laine
Perfect Tragedy by Jennifer Miller
Perfect Escape by Cary Hart
Perfect Summer by Bethany Lopez
Perfect Embrace by Kaylee Ryan
Perfect Kiss by Lacey Black
Perfect Mess by Fabiola Francisco
Perfect Excuse by A.D. Justice
Perfect Secret by Molly McLain

# ALSO BY MOLLY MCLAIN

## RIVER BEND SERIES

Can't Shake You

Can't Hold Back

Can't Get Enough

Can't Walk Away

A River Bend Wedding

Can't Resist Him

Can't Let Go

Can't Forget Her

## COLE CREEK SERIES

We're Made of Moments

More Than a Memory (December 2021)

## VELOCITY SERIES

Fly

Fight

## STANDALONES

Bend (Vegas Heat)

Rush

ACKNOWLEDGMENTS

First and foremost, I want to thank C.A. Harms for inviting me to participate in this incredible series! I had just announced that I was writing again after a couple of years away and being involved in the Mason Creek project has definitely helped me get back into the swing of things!

I want to thank the other Mason Creek authors, as well. Lauren Runow, A.M. Hargrove, Terri E. Laine, Jennifer Miller, Cary Hart, Bethany Lopez, Kaylee Ryan, Lacey Black, Fabiola Francisco, and A.D. Justice… You have all been a treat to work with, and I've enjoyed getting to know you all tremendously!

To Sarah Paige at Opium House Creatives… You nailed these covers and really helped us brand Mason Creek in the way it deserves. Thank you!

Much thanks to Ellie and Rosa at My Brother's Editor for their editing and proofing magic.

To Trevor Brachtenbach for his bull rider expertise. I'm so glad I didn't annoy the crap out of you, and I promise to give you more to do next time.

Huge thanks to Brittany Holland aka the Blurb Whisperer for her voodoo magic on my paltry blurb.

To Deb and Sandra for being my first Perfect Secret readers, and for giving me your ever-valuable feedback. Sandra, thank you for the ranch, cattle, and bull rider info, too!

To my bestie/sister wife Rhonda for always listening to my writing woes and for talking me off the ledge more often than I'd like to admit.

To my reader group, the Misfits. Your support along this journey means the world to me. I've said it before and I'll say it again—you're not just readers; you are friends, too.

Finally, to my husband and kiddos for your patience and love and support. We've come a long way and to think we've only just started again. I love you so, so much.

# ABOUT THE AUTHOR

Molly McLain lives in a tiny Wisconsin town with her husband, three kiddos, and two adorable German Short-haired Pointers. She's addicted to 80's ballads, 90's rock, cheesecake, and office supplies, and she's been scribbling down love stories in spiral notebooks since she was old enough to daydream about hunky boys and happily-ever-afters. Now she turns those daydreams into steamy, small town novels.